Praise for C

Kafka's Son

"By following a labyrinthian circuit—under the sign of Calvino and Perec—Curt Leviant takes us along the trail of Kafka. Breathtaking! ... As to whether or not Kafka had an heir, the answer is obvious. His name is Curt Leviant."
—*LIRE Magazine*

"A true literary success. Here Prague reveals itself as a magical, bewitching, mysterious, perplexing city. *Kafka's Son* is a fascinating novel that tempts you to take the first plane to Prague carrying a pile of Kafka's books."
—*Art Press*

"*Kafka's Son* is a realistic fantasy, a captivating maze, a detective novel, a love story, with multiple layers that never ceases to delight."
—*Magazine Litteraire*

"*Kafka's Son* is a work of genius."
—France 2 TV

"Leviant likes to captivate his readers, to dazzle them, to shake them off as he leads them deep into the recesses of his labyrinth, only to find them again unexpectedly."
—*Le Monde*

"With the genius of a Salman Rushdie, Leviant takes his readers into a kind of cinematic journey. He grabs the reader's attention and keeps him in suspense until the final page."
—*Soundbeat Magazine*

Diary of an Adulterous Woman

"Astute character studies drive this sexy, witty, philosophically complex novel. Without sacrificing humor or character development, Leviant manages to write an ingenious romantic farce in the tradition of Vargas Llosa's *Notebooks of Don Rigoberto*."
—*Publishers Weekly*

"Lots of fun. Leviant wanders into Harold Pinter's dressing room and ends up hanging out with James Joyce.... A comedy of errors as well as a bedroom farce—and much more."

—*Kirkus Reviews*

"Curt Leviant is a leading candidate for the title of best unknown American novelist....Compulsively readable and entertaining."

—*Sun-Sentinel*

"If Milan Kundera lived on Long Island, he might have written this novel, a meditation on love and intimacy. Like David Foster Wallace's *Infinite Jest* or Martin Amis's *The Information*, Leviant has put a post-modernist strategy in service of a character-driven novel with good results."

—*Library Journal*

The Yemenite Girl

"I read straight through without a stop. I don't often read so quickly and with so much interest. I enjoyed every turn of the story.... Shultish is a man with a life of his own...and the celebrity [the Israel Nobel Laureate, one of the heroes of the novel] too is marvelously drawn. *The Yemenite Girl* is done with great tact, feeling, and skill."

—Saul Bellow, Nobel Prize–winning author of *Humboldt's Gift*

"A passionate story...a true fiction.... The tension between the charm of the text and the intensity of the subtext is what keeps the pages turning."

—*New York Times Book Review*

"The best novel I've had the luck to review this year, and it may be the best novel many people will have the luck to read. In his first book, Curt Leviant has put together depth, delicacy, full-fleshed characters and gloriana.... The writing is rich and luxurious."

—*The Boston Globe*

The Woman
Who Looked
Like Sophia L.

Other Fiction by Curt Leviant

The Woman
Who Looked
Like Sophia L.

— AN EMAIL ROMANZA —

*ttt**

Curt Leviant

*transcribed, translated and transmogrified

DZANC
BOOKS

2580 Craig Rd.
Ann Arbor, MI 48103
www.dzancbooks.org

First US Edition: February 2024
ISBN 9781950539918
Jacket design by Steven Seighman
Interior design by Michelle Dotter

Library of Congress Cataloguing-in-Publication information Available Upon Request

This is a work of fiction. Characters and names appearing in this work are a
product of the author's imagination, and any similarity to real persons, living
or dead, is coincidental and not intended by the author.

Printed in the United States of America

10   9   8   7   6   5   4   3   2   1

*This book
is dedicated to
my editor and publisher
Michelle Dotter
with affection
and esteem*

In Lieu of a

Prolegomenon

As I STARTED WRITING this note preceding the romanza extravaganza, I recalled that the great Russian Jewish writer, Isaac Babel, would whittle down his fifty-page stories to ten; that Chekhov said, "I have a mania for shortness. Whatever I read—my own or other people's works—it all seems to me not short enough"; and that Saul Bellow, citing Kafka's brevity, agreed, adding, "We have no time. A good writer should write as short as he can." Then Bellow quotes a critic who says that books could be better by purging paragraphs of useless sentences and sentences of useless words.

So, then, I will compress Prolegomenon to Preface and ask my readers to write to me if they run across any useless sentences or words.

Purge "any" and change "run across" to "encounter."

To make it brief I'll say no more than—

Read on!

Change that to—

Go!

Is it possible for a story to have two beginnings?

As possible as it is for it to have two endings.

So I will share both with you, because for the life of me I don't recall which one really happened. When I think of one, I persuade myself, yes, this one happened. When I recall the other, that one jumps out at me, clear as a photo. Since all this took place a while back, when imagination and memory clash they yield havoc and confusion. You begin to believe in the reality of contradictories, the guiding principle of that definitive text, the contradictionary.

This is the way it began.

BEGINNING 1

ALL THE LOUNGE CHAIRS facing the water on the beach by Parma were taken, except one, next to a very pretty, actually quite stunning, blonde. Usually, when you read "blonde" you also read "young," but not here. Not this time.

She was about forty, with just the right mature good looks. Likely to protect her skin from the hot sun, she wore a light blue robe that both accented and complemented her lively green eyes. I noted too that a beautiful silk scarf of blended colors, chartreuse, orange, ultramarine, was lightly wrapped around her neck.

"Permesso?" I asked in Italian, pointing to the empty chair.

"It's all yours," she said, gesturing with both palms out, as if to say, no one's in it, you don't even have to ask. Her words came not with neutral politesse, but rather with a tone open and amiable, and with an engaging smile. She must have heard the English in my one Italian word, for her reply was in English.

I thanked her in Italian, "per la sua cortesia," sat down, took my book out of my little duffel bag and, after looking for a moment at the tranquil scene—sun and sand and almost still blue water—I began reading.

Given that warm welcome, I shouldn't have been surprised when I heard from her again.

"Sorry for interrupting you," she said in Italian, "but I can't help remarking, and it's really quite amazing, I also just began reading the very same Italian novel you're reading. *La Ragazza Yemenita*. What an exotic title."

"How did you come to it?" I asked.

"Saw a big ad in *Corriere della Sera*, one of the most important newspapers in Italy. Saw it was praised by the great American Nobelist, Saul Bellow. I love Saul Bellow. Any book he recommends must be a good book."

Since there is no "w" sound in Italian, she pronounced his name as Beloff.

"My Italian talking vocabulary is rather limited," I answered in Italian.

"I understand it, but I don't speak well."

"Seems to me you're doing very well," she said, again with a smile.

"Still," I said. "Perhaps English? And if not, then a bit more slowly, please."

She laughed, nodded, wrinkled her brows; she pursed her lips before saying in English, "Ah, okay, but the book you're holding, the *La Ragazza Yemenita* you're reading," and she pointed at it with a long, elegant forefinger, "is in Italian. So it is a puzzle."

She cocked her head, waiting for a reply.

I too laughed. She got me, I thought. "I know. I'm just looking at the Italian translation for the fun of it. You know the original is in English."

"I do," she said.

"Are you enjoying the novel?"

"I love it," she said. "Saul Bellow is right. I think this book is an immense novel."

I think she wanted to say "great" but erroneously used another word for size.

"Thank you," I said.

Now the woman gave me a half smile, half laugh. "Now I puzzled again. Why you thank me? For what? For what is the thank you?" But this time she didn't give me a chance to answer, for at once she said, "Since we are already in conversation, I think it would be polite to introduce myself. My name is Sofia. With an 'f.' What's yours?"

I wouldn't have told her on my own, but since she initiated the exchange, I had to tell her my name.

"But...but..." Her green eyes flashed as her forefinger began moving. Now she didn't just point. She kept jabbing toward my book.

Then it hit me. And only then. Not before. At first, who she resembled hovered like an attention-catching balloon floating before me. I wanted to seize it, but it was just out of reach. But then, as the balloon moved closer, the thought took on full shape. It happened the moment she tilted her head back when she smiled.

That did it. At that instant I saw in her face a legendary Italian movie icon. But of course I wasn't going to mention it. First, because a lot of pretty women here had that fetching south Italianate, olive-skinned visage. And second, because she probably had heard plenty remarks akin to: *You know who you look like?* But she wasn't a clone. There were differences, especially around the chin. Still, the resemblance was striking. I hadn't noticed this right away because I had first seen her as I looked down at her reclining in that lounge chair. And then, when I sat down next to her, I saw her only in profile.

It wasn't until Sofia faced me and I looked at her sloe eyes, those signature sloe eyes of the gorgeous world-famous star she resembled, those high cheekbones, that straight, slightly elongated nose with those flaring nostrils, those full, sultry, kissable lips, the lower lip a bit thicker than the upper, enhancing even more their sensuality, that I saw how much she looked like that film legend. But one generation younger. And then, the same name too. If Sofia were indeed a relative—all this still in the realm of fantasy: daughter perhaps?—then mother gave daughter her allure and her name, but with a slightly different spelling.

No wonder she said *Sofia with an "f."*

Of course, all of this is speculation, worthy of fiction. But sometimes speculation is more efficacious, even more exciting, than truth. Until confirmed, all this was just wild musing, pleasant but unsubstantiated (with fifteen letters, six of them vowels, the longest word I know) fun.

Sofia's "but, but" still echoed. I watched the rhythmic solo dance of her forefinger as she said, "But...but...you are reading...your... own... book!"

I could see how excited she was. Still, out of consideration and so that others wouldn't get involved, she spoke softly.

"Oh, my God," I said, closing the book, "I forgot it's illegal in Italy."

Again she laughed, but now she closed her eyes for a moment.

"No wonder you said *thank you*."

"It slipped out, believe me. I'm not the sort that likes to brag. I'm re-reading *La Ragazza Yemenita* because I know the story and it makes reading it in Italian easier for me."

"Well, about this roman you surely can brag." Sofia stopped for a moment and looked at me. "I can't believe I'm speaking to the author."

Now she swung her legs to the side of her chair and stood. Then she did something that surprised me.

"It's too hot for this," she said, her serious mien a contrast to her smiling eyes. Off came her sky-blue robe and silk scarf, both of which she tossed to the foot of her lounge chair. Then a swirl of orange hit me. I gazed up at her well-filled two-piece orange bathing suit. Saw heads turning. *Only teenagers wear such skimpy suits* went through my mind. A body just like her (presumed) mother's. From my reclining position I was at eye level with her tawny thighs. Not a drop of flab on her. Did she un- or disrobe once she realized who I was? I.e., did she do this for me? Or was it really too hot for her?

I must say all this was a rather pleasant feeling. It's always nice to be recognized, but when you're recognized by an attractive woman, the inner prize seems enhanced. And I wondered: can one be attracted to a woman just because she's in love with your book?

As Sofia bent down to pick up her lovely silk scarf, along came a sudden breeze and that scarf took off like an exotic bird. It flew like a little plane toward the water. I scrambled up quickly, gave chase. At first that sinuous scarf eluded me; it flew with a life of its own. But I finally caught it just as sand met sea, and I brought it back to her. Now we both remained standing.

"Thank you so much," she said.

"My pleasure. This scarf, it seems to be made of air. It's like a cloud in my hand. No weight at all...gorgeous," I said, not knowing if I meant the scarf or its owner.

"It is almost air. Actually, it's made of the finest, lightest silk."

For a moment there was silence. Only the swoosh of water and the occasional call of a child.

"Are you vacationing here?" Sofia asked.

Should I tell her I had been invited as a guest artist to spend a week here at the famous arts center, the Villa Due Ponti? No. I had shown off enough. So I held back.

"Sort of. And you?"

"I'm at the Villa."

There were three different small private villas facing the beach.

"Which one?"

"The one right behind us across the street."

"The Villa Due Ponti?"

"Uh-huh."

My jaw dropped. I know it's a cliché, but that's what my jaw did. That had never happened to my jaw. But this time it did. My jaw actually dropped and my mouth opened in surprise. Two coincidences in fifteen minutes.

Was Sofia in the arts too? If she were, she would have mentioned it. Could she be working at the Villa? With her elegance, she couldn't possibly have a menial job. And more, if her mother was who I thought she was, no chance she was a run-of-the-mill employee. Not with the upper-class élan of her face. Who knows, perhaps she was even the donor of the villa to the foundation.

"Me too," I said.

First Sofia's full lips pouted, then they slowly shaped a smile.

"No! If you're at the Villa, then you're here for something more than a vacation, so how come I didn't see your name?"

"I just checked in...and how come you're checking names? Are you the reservations manager?"

"No. No. I'm visiting my friend Renata here. She's the guest co-ordinator, and she lets me see which famous people are staying." She nodded thoughtfully. "Now I understand why I didn't see your name. You checked in after I left for the beach. I would have recognized it at once. Would you mind if I asked you a question?"

"Go right ahead, Sofia."

"Oh. So you remember my name. Very nice. I am pleased. So tell me, really. Why are you reading your own book? Do authors usually do that?"

There were loads of answers I could have given, some true, some fake, some imaginary.

"I do this to meet people. Like you. I meet a lot of beautiful wom-en this way. See? It worked. But really, I'm reading it to try to imagine what a reader feels like when he reads this book."

"Even though you don't understand what you're reading."

"I didn't say I can't read Italian. I just can't speak it well. And there are some languages I speak but don't understand."

Sofia pressed her lips and shook her head quickly. "This is too com-plicated for me. Only a writer can come up with something like this. Do you like your own book? Wait. I asked that already."

"I love it. In fact, I can't believe I wrote it."

Her reaction came like this: first in the sloe green eyes, then the smile, then a hearty laugh.

"You're funny, Giorgio. Like your book."

I tried to assess her amicability. Was she being polite or flirtatious? She did remove her blue robe to reveal her body soon as she heard my name, the author, the known writer. Or did she just preen for me? There is a difference, you know.

Focusing on Sofia, I hadn't paid attention to the seashore ambience. Now I did, breathing in the cool air. Blue-gray clouds, some shaped like birds in flight, moved westward. A faint taste of salt hovered in the slight breeze. I thought it odd, this mingling of taste and smell.

She looked at her watch and said, "I have to go now," with a little downturn to her lips, as if signaling her regret at departing.

As we were about to shake hands to say goodbye, Sofia went into her pocketbook, took out her phone, and asked for my email.

"I want to write to you," she said.

"I'll be glad to hear from you," I said. "So nice to have met you, Sofia."

"Me too," she said, "me too."

To preserve that amicable mood, I decided to depart a bit more intimately. I put my arms around Sofia, and she fell into that sudden, daring, impolitic, not-thought-of-in-advance embrace so naturally, as though we'd known each other for a long time and were good friends bidding each other not goodbye but au revoir.

Soon as my arms were around Sofia, I abolished time and duplicated space. Newton and Einstein would have been delighted. Maybe Poincare too. That time-space feat let me embrace two women, one with an "f," one with a "ph," who blended into one, as now and past elided. But still, my hands, be still my hands, my hands could not do what they would have done in dreams. Neither could my lips do what I fantasized. For I remembered a nice rhyme about politesse that my mother taught me long ago: "Even absent time and space, propriety still has its place."

The moments I held the two-in-one were long and short: enjoying the closeness of our bodies as if it was forever, yet aware of the quicker ticking of the clock.

Or maybe it began this way:

BEGINNING A

Fated?

Accidental?

Serendipity?

There are many words, some longer and longer (you've probably noticed the syllables increasing), to express the same idea.

I was on the Parma beach in a lounge chair reading a book and laughing.

I turned to my left, saw an attractive woman, eyes closed, sunbathing, wearing a well-filled two-piece orange bathing suit. At first a vague thought scudded, borders out of focus. Then it became sharper. This lovely woman looked familiar. But I was always seeing faces of people who resembled other people. She opened her eyes. Sometimes a person can feel another person staring and this makes one open one's eyes. I thought she'd say something. In fact, it seemed she was about to speak, then changed her mind. But I think that sparkle in her green eyes, overture to a remark, was still there. My gaze invited her, enticed her, gave her leave to speak.

It worked.

Soon enough she said something in Italian.

"Ho poco vocabulario per parlare italiano," I said, saying my Italian vocabulary was limited. "I can read but can't speak...English?"

"Certainly. For sure," she said. "I love that language. I can't help to comment. I see you really enjoy this novel you're reading. *La Ragazza Yemenita*. Laughing and laughing."

"How do you know it's a novel? Maybe it's a biography of Ezra Shultish, Hebrew scholar."

"First of all, biographies don't make you laugh," she said.

"Then I guess you haven't read mine. Read my biography and you'll laugh till you cry."

"Really? A biography of you? What is the title?"

"*A Funny Life*."

She tilted her head. "You're pulling my foot."

"Leg," I corrected, looking at her shapely legs. "Which isn't such a bad idea."

"You're funny. Like your book."

That took me by surprise. For a moment. Then I realized that by "your book" she meant the book I was reading.

"Funnier. And second of all?"

"And second of all, I know it's a novel because by incidence I'm also reading the similar book. And is making me laugh too. Isn't it nice when a un-animate object like a book can make you laugh?"

I sat up from my reclining position. "Sorry, but I hope you will forgive me, for I have to argue with you. To disagree. There is nothing more animate than a book. A book is not un-animate. It is quite animate. More animate than most people. The letters in a book breathe. They have a *vita*, a life of their own. I bet you don't know what words in a book do when you close the book."

"I don't. Do you?"

"No."

She laughed again.

"But I once heard," I continued, "that words in a book socialize. They read each other. It becomes a book that reads itself."

"That is quite amazing," she said. "A book that reads itself. And so the title of your biography, *A Funny Life*, fits you. But I suppose," and here she tilted her head flirtatiously, "I should know your name by now."

Now I could no longer resist saying it. And I said it. "But that's my nom de plume. My pen name. My real name is Giorgio."

At once her mouth opened and she said, "No! I don't believe it."

Now she sat up too and faced me.

"You're the author. Oh my God, I'm meeting the man who wrote the book that also I'm now reading, *La Ragazza Yemenita,* sitting right here next to me."

"And I'm meeting a reader."

She stared at the cover of the book with her big sloe green eyes. "Wait a minute. How do I know it's you who wrote the book? Anyone can hold a book and say, 'I wrote this book.' So how I know it's you?"

"Easy. Just look at my photograph on the inside flap." I gave her the book.

She turned the book this way and that, looked at the inside flaps.

"But there's no photo here."

"That's just my point. The no-photo looks like me. And if there *were* a photo it would look even *more* like me."

"Yes, I'm now concluding you wrote the book," she said. "You have the same beat-off humor."

I was tempted to correct her but held back.

As she lowered her eyes, I looked at her. She was probably in her early forties and radiated womanliness. She had long full sensual lips, a bit glossy from sunscreen, high cheekbones, bright green eyes at whose corners one could see slight hints of tiny lines forming—not a sign of aging but of maturity—and a fine, straight, slightly longish nose with enticingly flared nostrils. Her jaw was a bit full, a touch too wide. Suddenly, her eyes gleamed. A little smile, yes, a naughty one, danced in her eyes.

I caught that momentary sparkle and understood at once why it was there.

I was just waiting for the movement of her hands from her bag. It didn't take long. She burrowed into it and came out with a book. Purposely with the back cover up. And then, now beaming, she flipped it to the front and, as if presenting it to me, showed me my book.

"Are you enjoying it?"

I shouldn't have said that. What was she going to say, no?

"So, so much. By the way, my name is Sofia, with an 'f.'"

"So pleased to meet you," I said.

Sofia laughed. "Now come, really. If there would be a photo I would really, really know it's you."

"So you still don't believe me."

"Well, I do. But why no photo?"

"I don't like to publish my image."

Soon as I said "image" and looked at her, the image of the world-famous Sophia L. came to me. I don't know why I hadn't noticed before how much she looked like that Sophia with a "ph". But I wasn't going to say anything because she probably heard that often. And her body was also pleasingly formed. I know that sounds like a line out of a late nineteenth-century English novel, but I purposefully restrain my words.

Then occurred a little scene I'll never forget. Sofia noticed an older man peddling bottled water. He was bent over with his burden. She called him over.

"Signore, how much is one bottle?"

"One euro," he said, of course in Italian. "Four for five euro."

Sofia looked puzzled. "That's no bargain."

The man laughed. "Scusa, signora. My mistake. I mean five bottles for four euro."

Sofia gave him a ten-euro bill.

The man went into his pocket for change.

"Never mind, signore," she said. "The rest is for you."

After he thanked her and left, Sofia said, "I couldn't see that older man lugging that sack filled with bottles in this heat."

That moment etched itself into me. I was impressed by what a mentch she was.

It didn't take many more exchanges for me to learn that she was visiting her friend, the guest relations coordinator at the very Villa Due Ponti where I was staying.

"So how would you like to share a dinner this evening with the author of the novel you're enjoying so much?"

"You know, that would be a wonderful idea..."

Those words of hers sent a surge of joy thrumming through me.

"...but, unfortunately, in a couple of hours I have to fly down south."

"For how long?"

"A few days."

"Nuts. Too bad." I didn't hide my disappointment. "And I fly back home to the US day after tomorrow."

"So why don't you give me your email address?" Sofia went to her pocketbook and took out a little phone.

I dictated it to her.

"I would like to stay in touch with you, to write to you. To tell you something. Perhaps I could offer you some new material. It will be easier for me in the writing. Is that okay with you?"

"My pleasure," I said. "Too bad about this evening."

"Yes, indeed. But surely next time you come."

"By the way, I'm impressed that this is the first time you took out your phone. Usually, people are attached to it like a born limb."

"I'm not a slave," she said. "I don't know if you noticed but it has been shut off all the time. I direct it. It doesn't direct me."

"Bravissima."

She rose, took my hand and pressed it warmly. First with one hand and then, tenderly, with both.

Then something fascinating happened. She had been wearing a

lovely, light, beautifully colored silk scarf. As she spoke, she played with it, loosened it. Then came a sudden sea breeze that lifted it off her shoulders. It rose, took flight, hovered, seemed to descend, and then another gust of wind raised it higher. Meanwhile, I was moving, hoping to catch the scarf for Sofia. But then came a white gull, flying low and horizontal, that snatched the scarf and flew away. The rippling silk trailed after the white bird like a banner.

"Oh my," I said. "What a beautiful scarf."

"No worries," she said calmly. "I have quite a few others at home." She looked after the now smaller gull. "They make a nice couple. I hope they'll be happy together." Then Sofia turned to me again. "Now I have to go," and as she said, "Ciao," I watched her beautiful lips rounding the closing "o."

I stood and gave her a much better goodbye.

I took both her hands in a more than friendly gesture. Sofia smiled at once. It was a welcoming smile, that of a woman touching a man. The way I held her hands is worth mentioning. At first I clasped the four fingers of both her hands, a kind of modified handshake with a little extra man-woman energy. But then, and this pleased me, she took hold of my four fingers of each hand. For those who expect sexual miracles on an Italian beach encounter, this hand-holding may be light soap opera fare, but for a guy like me who analyzes the shift of molecules, this shift of fingers—Sofia's initiative; her move—was important. And I also noted that she wore no rings of any kind.

And this led me to do what I did next. I removed my fingers from her clasp and quickly put my hands around her back and drew her close in a warm embrace. Then quickly brought my face close to hers. Thoughts are now racing in my mind, parallel thoughts on little highways of their own creation. Thoughts shaped like questions: Should I bring my cheek to hers? Should I kiss her cheek? Should I bring my lips to her ears? And if I do, should I just press my closed lips to her ears? Or should I give her ear a light kiss?

There was another possibility, another deed concomitant to that hug. Kissing her on those inviting, sensual lips. That, I didn't even think of. Now that I reread what I have written I think I could have. Should have. And she would have welcomed it. But then I didn't think it would be appropriate. So I hugged her and she hugged me. And I pressed my cheek to hers and gave her a light kiss on her temple near her left eye.

The moment I held her, I rid myself of time. I was holding another Sophia in my arms. Everyone's dream. The past and now fused. I had abolished time. Time, but not propriety. I wasn't in a dream world. I couldn't do with my hands what they would do in dreams. Or with my lips what I was fantasizing. The moments I held her were long and short. I was enjoying the embrace as though it was forever, but I could hear the quick tick-tocking of the clock.

"I would love to hear from you," I said.

"I can tell by your writing that you are a very wise man."

"Well, it's not me. It's just a couple of my characters are very wise."

To this she said: "Professor Shultish and Bar Nun in the novel are wise and sensitive because the author has made them so."

And then we said goodbye.

That warm, womanly—I'd even say intimate—glow in her eyes when we parted, I still remember that.

And there is something else I remember. Sofia shook hands with me. But it was a handshake unlike anything I had ever felt. Perhaps unlike anything anyone else had ever felt, except in ancient myths or legends. I noticed that before she shook hands with me, she brought her right hand momentarily to her heart; then she pressed something warm into my right hand. For a second I felt something hot there. Then that sensation faded and whatever was in my palm was only warm. I bowed my head slightly, and she turned and walked away.

I opened my palm. A little flame, about the size of a marble, flickered in my hand. By now it was only pleasantly warm, not burning, not prompting me to quickly drop it. I stared at that small, gentle, warm flame, not knowing what to make of it. Then, suddenly, it vanished, like sunlight when the clouds come in.

But the warm, comfortable, intimate glow and the mystery of that flame remained.

All through the flight home, that warm-not-hot flame flitted in and out of my consciousness as I wondered what Sofia wanted to write to me about. Could it be a problem? But she didn't elaborate. If it was a problem, it's much easier to write than talk. With talking there is holding back, hesitation, even a desire to impress. With writing one can be open.

What kind of problem could this Sophia L. lookalike be having? Could it be her job? In fact, she had not mentioned a profession at all. Could it be health? She looked perfectly fit to me. Not an ounce of flab on her nicely shaped body. No, I wouldn't be the person to discuss health issues with. A woman like Sofia surely had, or once had, a husband. Perhaps she was now divorced or separated and wanted to discuss a problem with her ex. Or maybe it was another family concern. A feud with a brother or sister. Or a problem with a daughter or son. Maybe something with her mother. Maybe none of these. Maybe she would just share some new stories with me.

The only area I did not think of, probably because of the intensity of our first engagement, was the one outlined in one of her early letters to me.

And that little flame, surely a dream or a sudden spurt of imagination, me somehow extending the warmth of our meeting and conversation into a palpable warmth. For how can fire be transferred; a fire that does not hurt? And one that's only mellow, slightly warm. Where did it come from, that marble-sized little flame?

I should add that for a good part of our conversation Sofia was talking Italian to me and I was answering in English. I remembered that she said she would offer me some new...and the next word sounded like *materiale,* which in Italian as in English has several meanings: fabric, physical material, matter, and esoteric, non-touchable stuff like stories.

For a writer, new material is always intriguing, especially if presented by an attractive forty-year-old woman. If I were a tailor or designer, I'd also be delighted with new material. If a physicist, new matter would enthrall me. *Materiale* could also mean *things,* as in, *Hai materiale per scrivere.* You have material (pen and paper) for writing.

So then, Sofia's offer of providing me with *materiale* was a multidimensional play on words. She didn't realize (or maybe she did) that it struck home, for put into a query, "*Hai materiale per scrivere?*" besides meaning "Do you have pen and paper to write with?" could also mean, "Do you have material to write about?" And more: since in dialect *materiale* also means fabric (a coat made of fine *materiale*), Sofia would give me fabric out of which I could weave a story and, not being bound by her or my material—i.e., divesting myself of materiality—I'd enter the realm of dark matter, *materia scura,* and concoct a story out of whole cloth, using the finest *materiale.*

Wasn't it nice that Sofia was offering me both material to write about plus the pen and paper with which to scribe it?

So THEN, EITHER ONE or the other happened: Either

BEGINNING 1

or

BEGINNING A

As I said, I don't remember.

In the dream world we live in, likely both happened, because time is flexible, repetitive, and sometimes, like a bad watch, it also stands still.

June 24, 2017

Dear Giorgio,
It was a very special moment meeting you. Remember, I told you I'm going to write to you and share something with you.
I feel so honured to do this with a person of your reputation.
I'm very blessed to have crossed your path here in Parma.
It was a beautiful meeting.

Sofia

June 24, 2017

Dear Sofia with an "f,"
What a beneficent encounter. I would love to hear whatever you write. But in order for me to pay full attention to it, start your emails to me after July 14th, when I get home, as I am traveling now.
For me too it was beautiful meeting you.

All best,
Giorgio

June 24, 2017

Dear Giorgio,
Fine. On July 14th you will start receiving some of my writing.
Thank you for giving me the possibility to give light to something that has always been in the dark.

A presto,
Sofia

(NOTE: my comments on Sofia's letters will appear in this font.)

Some of her words puzzle me. I wonder what she means by "give light to something in the dark."
I got the impression she'd "share something" with me. Or give me some kind of "material." Another thing to wonder about.

June 24, 2017

Dear Giorgio,
PS. Writing back on same day. Sorry. Can't wait. Can't stop reading your book. Can't put down *La Ragazza*

Yemenita. The games the old writer, Bar Nun, plays with Shultish are so fascinating. Annoying the way he sometimes toys with him, but still fascinating.

Mi dispiace for not waiting a couple of weeks to write, but this letter is not about me but about your story.

Of course I can't be sure, but it seems to me you put yourself into that old Israeli/Hebrew writer, creative and smart, and also into Shultish, even though you will probably deny it, as all authors do, that the hero of a novel is based upon themselves, even though I know the rebuttal: that if you do that, do base it on yourself, that is if you do write autobiography, then you diminish the power of invention, but don't tell me that, and forgive this long sentence, Giorgio, for I bet that even in autobiography there is as much fiction as in a novel, if not more.

So not now, but soon, soon I'm so thrilled to share my love story with you.

WHAT?... was the word that shouted through my mind when I saw that four-letter word. First of all, shock. Banged on the head. I never dreamt she'd be writing to me about *love*. Second of all, for the tiniest moment, as long as it takes to say "love," I imagined maybe it was me she had fallen in love with. But then I told myself: face reality. If she really did like me, she would have let me know it in a different way, and not wait to announce it to me in a letter like a nineteenth-century heroine of a novel. So alas, she intends to write to me about love. Re: someone else. Not me. Me, I'd just be an outside eye, an ear, maybe a brain. And finally, and probably above all else, the question remained: How could a woman who looked like Sophia L. have a problem with love?

I keep replaying in my mind the fun I felt (is that correct English?) when you and I were in the same Villa Due Ponte in Parma a couple of weeks ago and I, by chance—but you, as a novelist will not say "by chance," you will say it was planned that way, destined, and maybe I'll agree—that I happened to come out to the beach from the same villa we were in, and we got to talking by virtue of your roman, and then I discovered who you were and I gave out a happy shout and said, "Oh my, you're the author of..." and I showed you that I, also like you, I too was reading your *La Ragazza Yemenita*, now isn't that destiny? I think it is, and too bad I didn't ask you to autograph your book for me. Hopefully, next time we meet.

Sofia

How could I say no? Even though I had no idea what she would be writing about. By now, all I saw was the word "love" in her letter. In all caps. And Italian. AMORE. In color too. Yellow. Also, I vaguely remember her mentioning the word "material." That's what she would be sending me. Here was a forty, forty-two-year-old woman radiating sexuality, very nicely shaped, with a know-it-all-ness in her big green sloe eyes and a slightly throaty voice, a memorable tanned face, the jaw perhaps a bit too square, but her ready laugh, smiling eyes, and warm demeanor deflected from this, and who needs perfection anyway? Once you have those big green cat's eyes, you're approaching perfection already. And a slow simmering fire in her, which, at the end of our encounter she shared with me by going to her heart and plucking out a tiny flame condensed into the shape of a marble that warmed my hand for a while, cool fire, but then disappeared.

And I ask myself when, not if, but when will I ask her if she's somehow connected to that Sophia L. whom she so much resembles.

July 14, 2017

Dear Giorgio:
You asked me to start writing from July 14th, so here I am with a brief email. Tomorrow I will send you couple of pages more I wrote. I am so glad you are willing to read, to listen to my story, which I will be sending you from time to time.

Remember, I told you I have a story about a romanza somewhat in the same vane like your *La Ragazza Yemenita*, you know, yearning for someone, which I would write to you slowly in the form of letters. And if I remember right, you said both "Sure" and "Of course." And that made me very happy, to have someone like you want to hear my story and take the time to read it.

That I don't recall at all. *At all.* And my memory is pretty good. It's not in Beginning 1, not in Beginning A. Maybe it's in the apocryphal Beginning 0.

Could I have missed mention of a parallel to my book? Could I have been so taken with her, the woman who looked like Sophia L., that I didn't hear the details re: a romanza, or had she *intended* to say all this but in the heat, the excitement, of the moment, simply forgot? And all I remembered was *materiale*? The answer is: no recollection of a story in the "same vane."

I am going to write to you about problems I am having regarding an affair with a man named Sandro, who is also like me married.

I met him in 2008 in a shop in Sicily, where both our families were vacationing.

I don't remember if I asked him about a certain item that was being sold there, or he asked me, but magically we were both attracted to each other at once. He is a tall, handsome guy who radiates immediate charm. Soon as I met him I realized it was him I should have connected with, not my husband.

A presto, and thanks again for your warmth and your enthusiasm, and I thank you again for your immense writing, which I am slowly enjoying day by day.

Sofia

Her letter stunned me. Stunned. That I never expected. Her to tell me a story about an affair. And both principal players married. I keep thinking about, expecting a continuation of the rapport we had established during our first meeting at the beach. But yet her "a presto" (see you soon) warmed me like that warm fire she had pressed into my palm, a gift from her heart.

And then another thought floated in the air like a solitary feather, like that lovely silk scarf that had sailed away from Sofia's neck which the gull nabbed in midair. I could not catch that feathery thought. It wasn't verbal; it was an image so fleet that, before you could really focus on it, it disappeared.

But, like writers say who want to give a hint of something but really intend to elaborate later—I'm getting ahead of myself.

I'll repeat what I said before. I could swear we had something with each other. I sensed the vibes in the air. You could snatch and seize them with five fingers. Too bad we're so far apart. I bet in person it could, it would, be different. I thought Sofia would say something like: *This is the story I wanted to share with you. I just couldn't tell this to you in person, but now via letter, I can. I am so attracted to you, just like your Ezra Shultish in La Ragazza Yemenita was drawn to the Yemenite girl. I started to like you via your book and then continued when, to my surprise, I found the author of the book I am reading and loving sitting right next to me on the beach.*

And is it only I who remember that little flame she gave me when she shook hands as we parted? Has she forgotten that? Is all that a dream? Like a light that vanishes with a click.

And now this. Telling me about an adulterous affair of hers. What a turn!

She did say before we said goodbye that she would be writing to me about a problem. But its depth and complexity are a surprise. Like out of a novel or a film.

Of course, I would continue to write to her. But to tell the truth, her obviously thorny romance with Sandro gives me some hope. So maybe there is a chance for my fantasy.

July 15, 2017

Dear Giorgio,
Anyway, today is the day I am really starting to write and elaborate to you my story. In fact, today Sandro turns 40. It is about time. You see, I'm 41, and we always joked

about the fact that I am in my 40s and he was still in his 30s. Thank god, now we are in the same decayde.

Stopped reading here...

15 luglio 2017

Dear Sofia,
Just walked through the door, it's very late at night, exhausted after a long, bumpy flight from London, and opened my computer and saw your letters, which I could not access earlier.
I was only able to read the first few lines. Want to focus on it, clear-headed, not half asleep.
Tomorrow I will read them slowly and carefully and respond.
So write everything, what is in your heart and elsewhere.

All good wishes,
Giorgio

And I continue to wonder. Sofia with an "f" is so beautiful, she's a creature out of the films like her lookalike, Sophia with a "ph," and probably so well-connected she could get any guy she wants, why does

she stick with a guy like Sandro, who has obviously been giving her problems?

Then the novelist who knows human nature in me suggests that
perhaps *because* of her possible (for all this is still speculation till I get
up the guts to ask Sofia outright) family link, she wants to distance
herself, declare herself independent, and make her own way, and not
rely on name, fame, to solve her problems.

We spent couple of hours together. A picnic on the hills
outside of Parma, some fresh bread and cheese and a
small bottle of vino. The birds, like *The Birds* of Respighi,
are singing on the distance. I'm so happy when I'm with
him. It feels so right. He just makes me feel complete. I
feel enflamed.

Soon as I saw that word, guess what happened? That little flame
Sofia had given me, and which had moved to the back of my consciousness, that little flame returned. Sandro gives her a flame; and
Sofia, whether she knows it or not, had given me a flame. I saw it,
watched it happen, she transferred it from her heart, to her hand, to
mine. And by so doing, she is also enflamed with me, I with her—at
least in some form of imagination or super-level of reality.

But on the other hand, tonight Sandro will have a big
party with his friends and his family. And this makes me
feel inexistent, mad, sad...even raged.
Not being there. Not being part of that life. His life. Out
I am left.

Amazing how quickly she switches. The "on the other hand" is the key to her entire relationship. The tottering bridge between "complete" and "enraged." It makes day night, black white, and up down. Mostly down. How can she even be continuing day after day like that? What kind of relationship is that? One that makes her enraged?

But this is my life with Sandro. Moments of pure symbiosis that alternates with other moments of solitude, anger and pain. OK, realizing this is one step in the equation. Call it the mental one. But action, the physical side, is needed too.

I decided to tell my story starting 2 years ago in 2015 when I have found Sandro again, after 9 years of silence. Of not being in touch for 9 long years. From then I will continue my story. Of course, I will also write about now, 2017, in Parma. But you will see it is not in chronological order.

Various countries will be mentioned in my letters, including Finland and Dublin and France and other places, and of course here in Parma.

I think I should tell you, dear Giorgio, that with Sandro it was attraction at first sight. Soon as I heard his low baritone voice in that shop where we met, something stirred within me. He told me later same thing happened to him. A wave of warmth came over him, rising from his midsection. In that shop he said something like, "Maybe we should continue this conversation over a cup of coffee," and that's how it started.

But there's no ending yet...it's still on the roll,

It's interesting that, likely unwittingly, Sofia is using an American gambling term, roll of the dice, to describe her relationship. Yes, her affair is a gamble. It's dicey. She's taking a chance. Anger and pain pressing down on a tottering bridge makes it more risky.

but I'm sure that you have already an idea in your mind how this should end. Right, Giorgio, who as writer is thinker too?

Indeed, thoughts about ending do run through my mind, not so much how it will end, that I do not know, although I can guess; but given the turmoil in me, I know how it *should* end. Reading those two "should end" words of hers, I joked to myself, Sofia knows exactly how it should end. A great difference between these two tiny monosyllables. Somehow in that sentence the dream wish words "with me" should be inserted, but then another dynamic, one that she doesn't know about, would be added to the story, another face to the mirror. Perhaps even another mirror.

I also marveled at the miraculous re-finding after a nine-year hiatus.

And where did she receive Sandro's letters? Surely not at home. Probably Poste Restante at her local post office or maybe at a POB.

Another thought re: those sad, potent, heavy words: "should end." Is that an invitation for me to edit her destiny? In a writerly manner? With a stroke of the pen? Or one on her cheek?

I don't know how detailed you want me to write, I have letters that Sandro wrote to me that maybe are worth to be shared with you.

It would be good to get another person's input and insight. Otherwise, I'm just reading her version of events. To this I'm not going to respond directly, lest I seem overbearing and intrusive. But if I'm going to make comments and assessments, shouldn't I know everything? No, just thought of it. I don't think I want to see his letters.

Do you want just a schema of facts or you would like also to hear about feelings, about more intimate details?
And last but not least how do I want you to see me? How you will interpret me from these pages??

Ah, here's an interesting opening. A little I-you, you-me link. The fact that she's concerned about how I might see her, judge her, brings me into her personal orbit. It's like a gentle, loving, press of the hand. This way I'm not just an impersonal, objective viewer of her story.

Luckily, I've met you, dear Sofia, I tell myself. Had I not, it would be difficult to make an assessment out of just reading words. This way I *see* you.

Anyway, this is my version of the story, knowing that there is no truth, just opinion.

What a marvelous line this is; it sounds like one by a famous philosopher.

I thank you again for taking the time to read my story.

A presto,
Sofia

I reply right away, but while I criticize the abrupt night/day, glad/
sad shift in her mood re Sandro, my own mood and manner of thinking is similarly split. In other words, the words I write are nowhere near
the thoughts I feel.

July 15, 2017

Cara Sofia,

I'm writing you soon as I got your letter.

I don't know who should thank whom more. It is I who
should thank you for confiding in me, for sharing your story.

Write with as much detail as you can. I want to know
everything. Curiosity may have killed the cat but it won't
harm me. I am inoculated against excessive curiosity.

So include facts and feelings and don't worry about
how I will "see" you. No matter what you say I will see you
beneficently, for you are a marvelous human being.

Tell me this and tell me that, and everything in between
this and that.

How and where did you get his letters? And where did
you re-meet?

Your story touched me.

Warmly,
Giorgio

PS There is no truth just opinion—what a brilliant
phrase!

Was I—yes, I was—talking out of both sides of my mouth when I said, "your story touched me"? It also touched a raw nerve.

And was Sofia also talking out of two sides of her mouth when she said, "It was beautiful meeting you"? Can one be a platonist and a romantic at the same time? That was my considered analysis. And hope. You see how a person can have conflicting thoughts at the same time. Arrive at a definitive conclusion about certain matters and at the same time hope it comes about.

Dear Giorgio,
Quick reply. Got his letters in a POB that I have here in town. We re-met on the express to Rome. Pure serendipity.

Sofia

I can't help playing with the last two syllables of "serendipity," which is what I feel for Sofia.

July 16, 2017

Dear Giorgio,

Before replying to your curiosity (which I love), which

I did not acknowledge, sorry, in that brief quick note I sent to you the other day, re: POB and where I re-met Sandro, I need to explain an antecedent...(isn't that a wonderful word?)

When I first met Sandro in 2008, like I told you last time, I was already married to Alberto, my first husband. Then I divorced and married a man from Finland.

Screwed the first marriage and, if I could, probably I would do it also with the second, my current, to Aarvo, who is in the silkworm eggs business, who I have to help at times. Maybe from outside people think of me as capricious, sentimentally inconstant. But I see myself as a woman who searched for love, lost it, then found it again... but maybe it was too late...

Anyway I'm sending you some pages...please tell me if my writing, my english is comprehensible and please forgive already from now all my mistakes (in all senses.)

Hope to read your comments soon.

Ciao,
Sofia

About my curiosity Sofia writes, "which I love." That word of hers resonates in me. I know she loves my curiosity, but her choosing to say she "loves" it, when she could have said she "likes" it, makes me think some special feelings are involved. It is an intentional word choice.

By saying, "forgive my mistakes in all senses," Sofia is apologizing not only for writing mistakes but also for life choices mistakes. She thinks I can help her with both. But the gorgeous woman who looks like Sophia L. doesn't realize what a non-impartial guide she's gotten.

I keep thinking about the resemblance. One of these days I'm gonna have to ask.

I wish I could write Italian the way she writes English.

So Sofia has had a lot of relationships. Alberto, first husband. Aarvo, present one, the Finn. Now Sandro, problematic boyfriend. One husband, a boyfriend lost and re-found, another husband she probably wouldn't mind losing. And perhaps other guys she has not mentioned.

Hard to assess what she means by "screwed." Screwed up, perhaps. She screwed up her first marriage and perhaps she wishes she could screw up her present one. But if that's what she wants, she's already on her way. For that she doesn't have to resort to wishes.

July 20, 2017

Dear Giorgio,
Sorry for this silence, days have been not long enough to do all the things I have to do...and writing needs time and concentration and unfortunately I'm lacking both at this time.
Now I'm in the train...going to Rome.
Yesterday I had a difficult day with Sandro. Difficult it's not the right adjective but I cannot find a better one.

She sure could have found a better adjective but she was too upset. "Difficult" is not the right word. "Awful" would have been on the mark, as soon becomes evident.

Sofia says she's on her way to Rome. But doesn't say why or who she's visiting. If her mama is the woman I think she is, I know she lives in Rome, so maybe she's going to visit her mother. Or maybe she's traveling on business helping her husband with silkworm eggs.

I had lunch with Sandro and the thought I had been creating of asking about us, took form

One of the clumsiest sentences Sofia ever wrote. Her confusion, her upset, spills over into her bad English. I think she wants to say, "and the question I'd been thinking of asking him about us took form."

Then I had a thought. Should I correct her occasionally awkward English or leave it as is to keep its authentic flavor? I decided to keep it as is and to continue to provide footnotes or comments for unclear phrases or passages.

and I finally asked him if we had a chance of a future together. I was so nervous asking this, like a kid in class hesitant to say something, afraid of being made fun, so nervous, I wonder if Sandro noticed the tremble in my voice. I had a lump in my throat—did he hear or see that?—and I in asking this crucial question I felt like an inferior daring to speak to someone in a higher station.

To tell you that the words I heard were not the ones I hoped to hear it's to make too easy.

I.e., would put it too simply, Sofia wanted to say. She's trying to express her complex feelings of disappointment and devastation.

Actually, I knew already what Sandro would say, deep down in my gut I knew, but it's always so painful to hear the actual words. Because it's one thing when you predict something (you can always be wrong), but when you hear it with your own ears that's another.

"Well, no," is what Sandro said. "Our love affair is confined to what it is and the thoughts of problems is bigger than the joy of living together."

And the problems we have are bigger than any joy, Sandro wanted to tell her. Or is Sofia just translating Sandro's good Italian into awkward English?

A black vale fell over my eyes. I think I passed out for a moment.

She meant "veil" but I thought of vale as the older form of valley and at once the expression "vale of tears" and the gloomy phrase, also so apropos here, "valley of the shadow of death" leapt before me.

I was very angry, I wanted to leave and scream. I could hardly eat and I should have told him to fuck off, but I was scared, too scared.

What's more, he told me something that hurt me very much: "Our love has small wings" which made me think of the tiny colibri,

Soon as I saw "colibri," I read "libri," the word for "books" in Italian. Co-books. Sofia and I were joining in books. I reread that previous sentence. Pure nonsense. Don't think I can't observe myself the way I can observe Sofia. I'm just looking for something, anything, to make a co-, a join, a link.

the little bird with tiny wings, the hummingbird, still it flys, still is beautiful.

But somehow I know he loves me. I am his love but he would not jepardize the stability of his family for me.

Re: the pathos, piteousness, and sheer sadness of that "somehow I know he loves me," I will deal with that later, down below.

It hurts. I cannot describe how much. I feel empty and suspended. My own small colibri/hummingbird wings clipped.

Tomorrow I will see him and I will write to you during the week end when I'm sure to find some time for me.

Sofia

PS Here's a story that might—will?—interest you. Once, during my first marriage to Alberto, I went, on my own, to see a psychologist, a self-styled marriage counselor.

As I said, I went alone, without my husband. This counselor happened to be Indian, from Bombay: Dr. Mahatma Jawarahal. He was nice. Understanding. We discussed music and literature, which I could not with my then husband. At least, this guy *listened* to me, not like Alberto. Then, after about three sessions, once, as I sat in my chair, he stood up from sitting behind his desk and walked to the other side of the room past me.

I did not turn. Maybe he had to go to the bathroom. Then he came to me from behind and suddenly bent over me and kissed me. I was surprised but, you know, I liked it.

He began calling me at home, on my cell phone, and I didn't dare do anything more with him than kiss him in the office.

But wait. Listen. There's a turn. Here is where the mundayn becomes memorable.

Listen to what happened next. That jerk apparently told, confessed to, his wife.

And then, one night...

Sorry to interrupt, stop here, but I just looked at the time and I got to pickup Neemi right now from a friend's house...Will continue....

Reading these words of hers, not her little memoir anecdote, but the important part that preceded it, her febrile, gentle, mousey reaction to Sandro's continuing insensitivity, I got the whole picture. My eyes saw, analyzed, consumed her letter. My eyes, they had ears, brains, all the post-evolutionary neurological accessories. They looked. Scrutinized. Absorbed. Understood. Everything.

At once. (It's almost as if her little psychologist story acts as a camouflage to reality.)

No longer was it snippets of letters I had to rely on. No need for that. I saw all the letters at once. And all were compressed by some mammoth scriptorium into four graphemes that used just three letters of the alphabet, two consonants and one vowel:

"Me" and "he."

And there were miles and miles to go between that "e" of "me" and that "h" of "he." A vast stretch of endless desert unbroken even by a prickly cactus.

Significant too is the pun value of the word "letters." Its two meanings. Her missives—and the discrete components of her words.

I could, but I won't, play with the double meaning of "miss" in missives and also with the other spelling and meaning of "discrete."

That pathetic reaction of Sofia's was a four-dimensional photo of her personality. And despite this fateful rejection she's going to see him tomorrow.

She's finished.

With Sandro nothing good will ever happen. He will pull her along, she will follow, sometimes on a high that makes her feel good for a moment, but always miserable when the inevitable lows follow. For when the multicolor illusory joy vanishes even denser and darker is the blackness. Gravitas to the grave.

That will be the only saving grace for Sofia. As I said above, that temporary high Sandro gives her, offering her the fleeting illusion—which for Sofia is real: illusion to delusion—that the "now" will become "will be." And then she opens her eyes to the real world.

Sofia says straight out that she wanted to tell him off with that common (and I mean "common" in all senses) four-letter word, the most often used monosyllable in the English language besides "and" and "the," but she was too chicken. There, in a nutshell, is her life. But if she stays in that frustrating, hopeless relationship with him, that moment frozen in time will repeat and repeat itself like a bad electric clock with a flawed second hand that constantly trembles vertically between twenty-nine and thirty.

Oh, my, what I could do with that phrase "second hand"!

And I will.

That's what Sofia is, a second-hand girlfriend, mistress, concubine, paramour, wannabe life partner. But never wife. A clock's second hand that jumps ahead, vibrates for a moment, and then goes back to its original position. Always pointing down, quavering, at 29 seconds after. A vibration, a tremble, that gives the impression of movement but actually goes nowhere. Like that damaged second hand, time will not budge for second-hand Sofia.

One would think that everything would fall in place for a woman who looks like Sophia L. That a woman with a face like hers would have no problems.

Then up pops the protective veil she drapes around that melancholic phrase, "Somehow I know he loves me..."

That's the gray illusory veil over her face, her life. Yes, the vale too. With the ominous shadow. But I won't share any of this with her. I'll have to ponder what to say. A gentle jab is better than a punch in the nose. So I wrote Sofia a brief, vague letter, told her I tried to call her but the line was busy. Sofia doesn't realize the funereal gloom that encapsulates that "somehow." Oh, the sadness, the clumsiness, the pathos of that "somehow," which she has no concept of, cannot read into, doesn't realize its import in her sentence. That "somehow" masquerades as joy with smiley lips that should be turned upside down.

Each letter of that crepuscular crutch of a word becomes fluid and starts dripping tiny drops of black ink, melting like Dali's timepieces in his iconic painting. That "somehow" stripped bare the essence of her worst day ever, when Sandro's words sent her to the vale of tears. But she clings on to that vertical, vibrating, going-nowhere second hand "somehow" as though it were the staff of life. That "somehow" makes me think of a person trying to cling to a glass wall with fingernails.

July 20, 2017

Dear Giorgio,

So happy to read you and to know that you tried to call me. I'm so sorry I missed your call.

You know what? I re-read my letter and I was hit by the words "love affair." It jarred me. To my mind, mine is a love story and not an affair. I don't have the feeling of doing anything wrong, just persuing happiness with the man I love....just forget about the rest. For me the word "affair" has a connotation of sin, guilt, and I don't feel a sinner nor guilty. If I feel guilty of anything I am merely guilty to have let Sandro go, when it was the right time to keep hold of him. Then we could also analyze the word "right."

Anyway a thought it's floated in my head since yesterday. Or maybe it's not a new thought. I think that when it *was* the right time, Sandro never made a strong move to have me. He is always been "cautious" with me...He told me yesterday that he tried to get the love of his life but I was hard to catch...

There! There's another bold face key to the entire relationship. Even years back Sandro made no bold moves to take Sofia away from her husband. He was quite happy to have an affair. And he puts the blame on her.

It seems, then, he is trying to suggest I was slippery, but it is *his* remark that is slippery.

There will be more explanation, be reassured...but for

now I had to write what was on my chest.

I go to bed now and let myself cuddle in the arms of Morpheus.

Thanks for being there and for reading me.
Sofia
Maybe I'm

I'm, what? What a typo! How many different ways there are to finish that phrase she left hanging in the air. And look in whose arms Sofia is cuddling when she goes to bed at night. Not in husband Aarvo's Finnish arms. But in those of the mythic, equally slippery Morpheus.

PS
Little story. Last night, with pre-arrangement, I went out for a little walk and met Sandro for a quick hello. We talked about his vacations and he showed me some photos he took with his blackberry. Sure enough there was one with his wife alone.

Does the word "with" = "of"? If it means "of," then Sandro took a picture of his wife. If "with" means together with his wife, then someone snapped just the two of them posing together.

And I asked Sandro without even thinking, it just popped out of me, had I thought about it perhaps I wouldn't have asked it. But because I was so annoyed, so hurt, I *did* ask, "You take pictures of her??" And Sandro answers

at once, quite simply, completely unaware of how annoyed
I am, "Si, ogni tanto." Meaning, "Yes, sometimes."

A black curtain, like I was suddenly dizzy, comes over
me. I am so pissed off.

But what do I do? I get so reaking jealous!

"reaking" is obviously a typo. Sofia forgot the "f," a powerful con-
sonant for her. The first letter of what she should have told Sandro to
do. And again she blacks out. Faints for a moment. That black vale.

Ok pictures with kids—but her alone?

So it *is* a photo of Sandro's wife alone. He's not posing with her.

And if he does take a photo of his wife why he has to
show it to me? Or does he show me her photo so I can see
who my competition is? The woman I'm screwing while
her husband is screwing me?

That word hit me as if it were an object. A missile. First time she's
been so direct, so open, about her affair.

And by him taking a picture of his wife, what the hell
does it mean?? It means that he cares! That's pretty obvious, isn't it? He cares.

Of course he does, runs through my mind, but I am not going to tell her this. At least not now. Sofia doesn't realize it, but she is revealing, step by step, the doomed history, the non-progress of this affair, which will never go anywhere. Still, Sandro photographing his wife could also be interpreted positively: as a pretense on his part, a make-believe. And if Sandro had any brains, he could have told Sofia, "I'm doing this as a ruse to waylay suspicion. That's why I'm taking pictures of her."

Fine, that's good, the picture taking, vis-a-vis her, Sandro's still-unnamed wife. But how about Sofia? Her question is still valid, potent too: why should Sandro show that photo to Sofia? She is absolutely right to (f)reak out. That guy is either a jerk or thoroughly insensitive. Better yet: an insensitive jerk. He has to be a jerk not to seize and hold on to a gorgeous woman who looks like Sophia L. And what's more, he's probably not even on par with her intellectually. I have a hunch his cultural level is a notch or three below hers. Sofia never told me what he does and I'm not going to ask her. He's probably some careful insurance type. Good looks cast a vale over all defects.

That "ogni tanto" of Sandro's stressed me out. That means he takes those pictures of her more than once. There is, there has to be, something intimate in taking a photo of a wife. The pose, where waves of warmth, smiles, intimacy vibrate between posee and photographer. To take a photo of a wife cannot simply be a cold click-click experience.

Dammit! Why do, did I, let myself in for this?

Absolutely right! Why do you, Sofia? You naïve, love-hammered woman.

Maybe there are degrees of love and he loves his wife dearly and he loves me passionately, but is it enough?? Can it be enough for me?

You can't split love. It's not an apple or an atom. And you know what happens when you split an atom.

꩜

July 20, 2017

Dear Sofia,

I am interrupting the reading of your letter to answer you right away.

I have a different take on Sandro's "solo" photo, from a writer's point of view, a man's point of view, an amateur psychologist's point of view—all of them mine.

I.e., it's a little bit more optimistic than your reading of it.

And that is: It is also possible that Sandro took this photo of his wife to allay suspicions. By taking a photo of his wife he "shows" her that he cares to have a solo photo of her, and by so doing he lets her assume that she, like solo in the photo, is the only one. I think if that is his intent, it's a clever ploy. And if I were writing a story from Sandro's point of view, a photo like that would be just the thing to do.

All best,
G

PS. Why haven't you sent me the continuation of that fascinating Indian marriage counselor story?

July 20, 2017

Dear Giorgio,
I am answering you at once.
Thanks so much for writing back. And in mid letter too.
Regarding your interpret of Sandro's solo photo taking of wife: I never thought that a man like him could be so Machiavelic in his intent.
Surely I don't recognize Sandro setting up such a ploy.
But maybe I don't know how man think and maybe I know less than what I like to believe of this man.
I think, without deep interpreting, he just wanted to take that photo and he did.
I guess that is more simple, more straightforward! But problem still is: why show me?
Still, somehow your thought and point of view made me smile!

Best, and thanks so much,
Sofia

PS. Sorry, here is more of my Indian story. Shows you what a "great" editor/writer I am. So I am now continuing the tale about the dumb psycho who must have told his wife that he was kissing one of his patients...

So, then, one night, probably a couple of days after my most recent appt with him, there's a knock on my door. I open it and there, in a jealous rage, the man's wife burst into my apartment, dragging the psychologist with her, and told my husband:

"Do you know what your wife is doing? While consulting, getting advice from my psychologist husband? She's kissing him."

This news devastated Alberto and he began bawling like a baby, despite my yelling to the wife, "It's him who snuck up on me and began kissing me! Why don't you ask him that, you moron, before you make accusations and bursting into my apartment?"

And Alberto stormed out.

But wait. Story not over yet.

Tell you next time. For that photo of Sandro's wife is still bugging me.

Baci,
Sofia

(Sofia's previous letter, continued:)
Another PS. Sure enough this morning I woke up very early and my stomach is in nots,

A wonderfully Freudian typo. Nos and nots are pervading her. This love is not for her. Skimpy on yeses, full of nots. Every action of Sandro's ties her into nots.

entirely upset. Just for a picture that reminds me of the brutal reality. Like a slap in the face, which I should have given him. And then once and for all he would have known my feelings.

Yes, indeed. Should have. Which her life is a bundle of: should haves.

But who knows, perhaps that would have driven him away? A slap is a rather daring, extraordinary gesture between lovers. The brutal reality is: he has a wife.

A wife whose photo haunted me last night in my dreams.

Why did Sandro have to take that photo? And show me. It's like sticking a needle into me. What was the point of showing it to me?

Is he that naive? Simple-minded? Or does he, for unknown reasons, do it with malice aforethought? And worse, why does *he carry that photo with him* like a talisman, ready to show anyone: wanna see my wife?

So this photo of Sandro's wife had its effect on Sofia day and night. How much more damage can Sandro do to Sofia before she realizes she must say goodbye? That's another thing I forgot to consider. Not only does Sandro take the photo but he carries it around with him. That's a bit harder to give a positive spin to. Earlier she can't imagine him so Machiavellian; now she wonders if he did it with malice aforethought. Poor Sofia is always split.

And that callous "Si" of his may be the tipping point. Maybe I should put a "r" between the "t" and "i." The tripping point, the turning point, in the Sofia-Sandro alliance.

If she's already playing with letters—she's catching it from me—I'd start the last word of her sentence with a "d."

You see, dear Giorgio, I'm really thinking in, living in, English. But I'm still hesitant to use the words "love affair."

This afternoon my good friend Viviana that lives in London is coming to visit me.

I took 2 tickets to go to see Roberto Benigni interpreting the *Divina Commedia*, Canto XI. It's all about Hell. You probably saw his touching film about a concentration camp, *Life is Beautiful*, for wich he won Best Actor in the Academy Awards.

I don't know if lovers are in this canto. But I told Sandro, last night, that for sure we will burn in Hell.

He shook his shoulders,

shook = shrugged

in a gesture that seemed to say, I don't care, looked at me, then said an abrupt, "Yes."

That was another remark I didn't want to hear. I wanted him to disagree with me. To make me feel less guilty. Less sad. To console me. Cheer me up. Not that brusk "Si." Telling me, yes, you're absolutely right. Right to Hell

is where we'll go.
    But it's all from this side of the world,

Very enigmatic line. Notice, it ends with a comma, not a period. What does she mean by that? Maybe she means that all her remarks are one-sided. That her words and views are coming from one side. Hers. Not his.

And then, in the very same line, right after the comma she glides right into my book.

still reading and loving your *La Ragazza Yemenita*. I hope next time I see you you won't forget to sign it for me.

Baci,
Sofia

Sign it, she writes. Hopes to see me again. Shall I interpret her "Baci," kisses, analyze it the way she analyzed Sandro's showing her his wife's photo? Is this an obligatory closing to a letter? Or are these kisses more personal? Although my face is as mute as the face of Friday, Robinson Crusoe's pal, my heart gets pumped up, the rest of me too, excited, when Sofia complains about, criticizes, Sandro. When I reply to her this time, I'm not going to hold back. I'm going to tell her straight out what I think of Sandro.

Re: the top line of the letter, where she writes "read you" (right after Dear...)

Sofia makes "read" a very transitive verb, with me as a direct object, "so happy to read you," like "hold you," "kiss you," "caress you."

And later in the letter she makes herself the direct object, "thanks for reading me." Maybe it's widely used in Italian, but I've never encountered that usage in English. And what a PS! Not a letter but an entire narrative, richer and more detailed and much more revealing than the regular letter above it.

I guess Sofia took my ambiguous words as a kind of encouragement—I think I used the phrase "time will tell"—but frankly I don't know what I would have said to her had she answered the call. I probably would have been more direct. Would have asked her to assess her feelings at the moment she said,

"I should have told him to fuck off." But I will assess her feelings as only an objective person like me, straitjacketed by overriding subjective emotions, can. She's on a yo-yo, going up and down, occasionally way down, as witness her barroom talk. In my view, Sofia's relationship with Sandro is so tenuous that any excessive vibration in that yo-yo cord can bring it down completely. And her tie to husband Aarvo is so weak, she hangs on to any hope of being loved, even if she's constantly slapped in the face. Which she hesitated to do to Sandro.

Regarding that show with Roberto Benigni reciting from Dante's Eleventh Canto, Sofia writes only about Sandro's nonchalant shoulder-shrugging re burning in Hell. Listening to that Canto at the theater, she must have felt awfully uncomfortable. I looked into the *Commedia* and saw that Dante talks about false lovers and hypocrites, frauds who live in the Eighth Circle of Hell.

If that didn't nudge her to break off with Sandro, what will?

Did I want to see a photo of Sandro? No. And Sofia never asked me if I wanted to see an image of him, and I never suggested she show me one. I certainly wouldn't want a photo of him stuck to my consciousness every time I pictured their affair. I'd rather have a no-image in my mind's eye than a real one. A vague, fuzzy outline would suffice. And it never even dawned on Sofia that both her name and her boyfriend's name begin with the same letter. She could have made something of that. Or maybe she realizes and it's too banal for her.

That serpentine S.

Two serpents looking for the elusive Garden of Eden.

One day it dawned on me: could Sofia be teasing me? Detailing her romance with Sandro as a way of saying, look how desirable I am? Doing her June Parma beach orange bikini routine for me now with words instead of a swoop-swoosh of a cerulean terrycloth robe? Can one convey a surreptitious allure via emails? On the face of it, it didn't seem she was purposely luring me on. Dangling me. For her emails expressed straightforward appreciation of my comments. With absolutely no—to use her words—machiavelic intent. Not like me, who when *I* wrote to her, *I* was split in two. My forked pen, i.e., my keyboard, said one thing while my heart/mind was thinking another. Two trains running on parallel tracks. The old story. The left hand doesn't know (or at least pretends not to know) what the right hand is doing. One's bottom half with a different agenda than the top.

Wait a minute, I said to myself. The lines in the paragraph above sound familiar. Heard, seen, them before. Deja vu. Then I realized I was quoting myself. Never done that before. Copying lines, reciting them like a schoolboy, from a book I was now writing.

And then I wondered, wandered, even further. Is it possible that Sandro was made up? All this just to keep writing to me? Quite imaginative to create such a chap in her emails. And if so, why invent him with a problem? If he was a fantasy, she would have made up a happy encounter. No one would concoct a continuing open sore.

No.

Bottom line.

Sandro is real.

[decorative ornament]

July 21, 2017

Dear Sofia,

Painful words to read, but words such as yours continually repeat themselves in the history of love affairs. They are like a universal refrain in international love songs, songs that bemoan an affair gone wrong.

I hope you know what the expression "mince words" means—when you hold back the words you really want to say and instead substitute more gentle words.

So I'm not going to mince words in my reaction to what happened to you.

In short: what you've described about Sandro and his behavior toward you is not only unacceptable, it is awful. It's a shame.

Shameful. Absolutely shameful.

A disgrace.

Mean.

Self-centered.

You asked me to comment and so I am commenting, with absolute honesty and directness.

His behavior is not only totally inconsiderate, it is awful.

I'm writing it again. Awful. Mean. Shameful. I'm sorry to say this, knowing how much he means to you, but I have to say it.

No, that's not true. I am not sorry to say that at all. It's me (or is it I?) who is mincing words. Not only am I not sorry to say Sandro is inconsiderate, I'm rather happy to express it. Absolutely delighted.

I have held back till now, dear Sofia, each time telling myself, I don't want to hurt her. But I have come to the conclusion that I am hurting you more by keeping silent.

I can't let you continue to live in a fool's paradise any longer. So then, I'm sorry to have to tell you what I really feel.

Sandro doesn't behave like a lover. Shall I tell her to tell him, the way she wanted to, but held back, to fuck off? I'm not quite ready to do that.

Yet.

And as I write, I dream, fantasize, peel the weeks away into the fall.

Have I mentioned to Sofia that I plan to come to Italy in the fall?

Thinking of her and her adulterous romance, I muse: will I ever be able to write up Sofia's fascinating story?

In fact, as my pen shapes the serpentine "S" of her name, I already have the title of my unwritten romance. Unwritten, yes, but in my thoughts rehearsed, imagined, and already rough-drafted.

But that "S" of hers prompts me to recall the phrase re the two serpents in the elusive Garden of Eden.

It's me who's writing like a serpent, saying one thing but really meaning another. Pretending to sympathize with her but secretly, serpently rooting for the success of Sandro's double dealing, hoping for the day the words she should have said, could have said, wished she'd had the guts to shout, that two-syllable, two-word phrase in street lingo lurking in her heart but stuck in her throat.

Another instance of serpendipitous linguistics, a meaningful homonym:

I call Sandro "mean" and then I tell Sofia, "how much he means to you."

How with an adroit leftward chess move of that significant letter "S" plucked from one word and inserted into another, one can easily change the meaning of that sentence to reflect Sofia's reality: how much he's mean to you.

Called you again today, 5 pm your time, but your "voice" told me you were on your way to Rome.

All best, so nice to hear from you; reading your words it's as though we're speaking to each other.

Baci,
Giorgio

July 21, 2017

Caro,
PS to a previous letter. Just reread it.
Funny that the words "maybe I'm" remained there like suspended...
Forgot to finish, May I'm....
Reconsidering, don't know how to finish it.
I'm?? What am I??
I will try to answer that question...
Maybe I'm just human.
Ciao, Giorgio, take care.
Looking forward to your reaction to that letter.

When she wrote the above PS, she evidently had not yet gotten my long letter.

She used "finish" twice. She's probably thinking in Italian and so doesn't realize the pun value of that word.

July 21, 2017

Dear Sofia,
It's you who has to take care. You're like a blindfolded youngster spun around two or three times who has to walk on a diving board.
Surprises lurk.
The depth beckons.

Yours warmly,
Giorgio

PS Can't wait to read end of your psychologist story. Send it!!!

Too late. After sending the above note did I realize the gravity, the ominousness of my words. But who can plumb the depths—again that word—of the unconscious.

Likely I wanted to say those portentous words for reasons of my own.

July 24, 2017

Caro Giorgio,

So sorry I missed your recent call, again, but strangely your email was missing from my phone. It's now back in securely.

Your words mean so much to me and exchanging thoughts with you it's such a privilege. And of course I appreciate your heartfelt and deeply moving letter, full of your big-hearted feeling concern for me.

No wonder you're such a good writer, dear Giorgio. You have the capability to analyze each word, even each letter.

After dinner here in town I went to the book store to search for the new Italian translation of Dostoevsky's great novel, *Crime and Punishment*.

The title is so apropos, don't you think?

Unfortunately I was sold out...

Went again this morning to another book store and found the book.

So this novel and also *Decameron*, along with your *La Ragazza Yemenita*, will come on vacation with me in south France...I'm in good company....

Bacio,
Sofia

PS Here's the end of the story. After the Indian and his wife left, the following took place the next morning. Walking in town—the wife must have come early to my street and watched me leave the apartment house—while I was crossing a small street, I saw a car bearing down on me. By a hair I jumped away in the knick of time, and I saw the face of the driver: the psychologist's wife, trying to take her revenge.

What a story, but frankly, I expected more of a reaction from Sofia re: her Sandro problem, after my long letter. She offers just a couple of lines of appreciation and then segues into dinner.

Am I getting through to her?

Usually, I'm the one who is traveling, but now it's my book traveling—with her, and probably at night it's right next to her on the night table. Maybe she dozes off reading and my book lies flat on her breasts. Here's one time I would have wanted my photo, which I never include in any of my books, on the back of the dust jacket. It's me, not *La Ragazza Yemenita*, who should vacation with her.

A few lines up, another great Freudian slip. Prophetic too. Fatidic. Always wanted to use that word. Sofia meant "it," but writes, "Unfortunately, I was sold out..." But maybe there's no such thing as typos. Maybe deep down she *meant* to say: I was sold out. Sold down the river with her hapless love affair. But she probably doesn't know that Americanism, "sold down the river."

She's continually being sold down the river by Sandro and thinks she's floating on a kayak, which, like its palindromic structure, goes back and forth but gets, arrives, nowhere.

With Sandro in a café

Dear Giorgio,

Here's another story for you. I guess this scene could also be in a movie, or in a novel. I am sitting in a cafe having a coffee with Sandro, when into the cafe, to my astonishment, or surprise—I know that Samuel Johnson wrote, or said, a witty description showing the difference between the two words—not seeing me first...

Like a good storyteller, I am going to give you suspance, and you guess...

Who could it have been? Obviously, someone she knew, and hence didn't want to be seen. So it's either her present husband or her former husband. Or, maybe, Sandro's wife. But Sofia doesn't know her. In that case, Sandro should be surprised. Or astonished. Not Sofia.

Got it! Sandro has just come into the cafe. Wait a minute. That won't work. Sandro is sitting next to her. So I write back:

Dear Sofia,

Both husbands enter. To your great surprise. Together.

Giorgio.

July 29, 2017

Dear Giorgio, (Will continue the "movie" story later.... Meanwhile...)

I'm sitting on a bench here in Nice.

But I'm sad and frustrated. I shouldn't be, the weather is good and I'm on vacation. Still I'm sad and angry. I don't want to be here, and yet I don't want to be anywhere else.

I just feel disconnected with everybody.

Many reasons for feeling like this. Maybe I should not have said loud to Sandro that I wanted out.

July 29, 2017

Cara Sofia,

Hold it. I'm interrupting the reading of your letter when I see these words:

"I wanted out."

When did you say these words—**"I want out"**—to Sandro? That's news to me.

Never saw those words in print.

Giorgio

Caro,

I wrote it, briefly, in my last letter. It didn't get to you?

Sofia

So maybe my long letter did have some effect, if indeed after getting it she told Sandro she wants out.

(Sofia's letter continued:)

I'm scared that my words are somehow creating that reality. I'm scared of this "want out." But tell me, in two days he could not find the time to send me a message??

Ok he is on vacation too but if you want to send a message you find a way. Right?? How can I be so stupid and letting him and a damn message ruin my day??

I'm smarter than that?? Or maybe not?

You know I'm not behaving nicely. I'm letting all my resentment out on my family.

Maybe I'm not the open-minded, full of life, smart, funny woman I pretend to be??

Cara Sofia,

Again I interrupt the reading of your letter to quickly tell you that you are smart.

It is just that now the emotional part of your brain is overwhelming the thinking part of your brain.

When and how did you tell Sandro you wanted out? In

person? Phone?
   Email?

   She wrote back at once, but her reply was so muddled—she must
really be in a tizzy now—that it was hard to penetrate. It seemed it was
done over the phone, but I'm not sure, and I'm not going to pursue it.
The very fact that she planned to say it and did say it shows she's going
in the right direction.
   Again she's criticizing him and herself too. Not a happy combo.
For by doing both she can't move forward resolutely.

   (Sofia's letter, continued:)
   I'm more full of anger and pity for myself. I don't like
me right now.

   Cara Sofia,
   But I do ! ! !
   Right now.
   And before.
   And tomorrow.
   There. I have used up all three time zones.

   Giorgio

She not realizing that I mean more than I say. And she writes back quickly:

> You're so so so sweet, Giorgio. Bacio. *Bacio*. **Bacio.** One for each tense.
>
> Thoughts can be changed fast. I could switch to a positive way of thinking. Enjoying that I'm alive. And today it's a new day...Damn, why I can't do it??
>
> This is not the Sofia, full of joie de vivre, writing to you, but I don't want to hide her to you so that I make a good impression. The story and the person are one, you told me. She is also part of me...part of the story.
>
> I got married 10 years ago, in Dublin, Scotland. We had just met 6 months before. Aarvo was 1 year older than me. Finnish. With a tiny part Swedish.
>
> But somehow he seemed so connected to family I almost sensed a stranger. And this tested my already precarious self esteem.

Another of Sofia's loopy sentences. I think she wants to say, Aarvo was so family-oriented that with his family she almost felt she was a stranger.

And for a moment I become her, feel her dolor. But at the same time another feeling, vague and slippery, was also hovering over me. Then it slid in.

How romantic. A hot-blooded Italian woman who looked like the sex goddess known all over the world, with a northerner, an icy Finn.

I could imagine the arctic fireworks between them. Too bad he wasn't from the Netherlands, then I could have had him spending most of his life below water, his fingers on his dyk.

She got married in Dublin, Scotland, an alternative dream city built by Italian citizens seeking quick marriages.

Cara Sofia,
This is such an unusual letter. Writing to you so many times in the middle of the reading.
But then I thought, all this is like kissing a girl through a thin silken kerchief. Something of essence is lost.

Sofia, thinking in Italian, is writing in English, conveying what her husband, Aarvo, thinking in Finnish, and speaking a fractured Italian, had told her years ago, words that may have shifted slant over the many moons.

I almost sensed a stranger, you write. Maybe you mean "felt" instead of "sensed." You felt like a stranger.

Giorgio

(Sofia's letter, continued:)

Words can hurt more than a punch. But this was long ago. But still I believe it.

Aarvo is writing a book about his business, silkworms and their eggs.

I thought that maybe you could read the book. Give your precious advise. Then I thought I did not wanted to share you. Don't laugh. Exclusivity. That's something important to me. It's childish I know. All relations are different. Because the people relating to it are. So what I share with you, what we discuss, it's ours no matter id you read or not Aarvo's book. Right?? Don't laugh.

So would you like to read all about silkworms?

Oh well I hope my next email will be more?!?! Ok it will be different.

Ciaoooo

Sofia

"I did not wanted to share you." I liked that phrase. Amend that: I didn't like it. I loved it. Here again flowed, floated, that vague, pleasant feeling. A sense of one-to-one ownership, as if mysteriously we were linked and I wasn't just a conduit for her confessions. Sofia doesn't wanted to share me.

And the words "share" and "you" and "ours" also reverberated warmly in me. I think I should say that by now I no longer thought of Sofia conjointly with that other Sophia with a"ph" as I did when I first met her, thinking that when I hugged "f" I was embracing "ph" as well. Now Sofia stood solo in my mind, and when I mentally embraced her, it was Sofia alone.

That "id," another great Freudian typo for "if," which came right after "ours," also reverberated warmly within me. And that "id" in "did not wanted to share you" did not escape me either. Id is psychic energy; that's me. Id is also the pleasure principle; that's her, Sofia, following the ideas of the philosopher Epicurus to their height.

Dear Sofia,
No, I don't think I will read about silkworms. If it's fiction, yes.

Giorgio

With Sandro in a cafe

Dear Giorgio,
Continuing the cafe "movie" scene.
You said both husbands enter, to my surprise.
So you are 50% right. But which 50%?
Tell you later.

Sofia

With Sandro in a cafe

Dear Sofia,
A wonderful, suspenseful story. So which one is it?
The current one?

G.

Caro Giorgio, (Re: cafe story; that one will continue)
I loved that line in your recent letter, kissing a girl
through a thin silken curtain. It's so beautiful. So original.
So you. So full of fun, humor and wit.

Sofia

Important PS Speaking of humor and your questions re: Sandro. You have made me look into a window I have never peered into before. I just realized
from your question asking me if Sandro has a sense
of humor. I never thought of it till now. And after thinking of it, I must say that he does not have a sense of
humor. I cannot think of one funny thing he said, so I
guess when we laugh it's about something I have said.
Been busy with other problems to even consider that is-
sue. Yes. It is too bad.

Just as I thought. A man totally devoid of humor. How can she love anyone without a sense of humor? How can one live a life without laughter?

Dear Sofia,
In other words, he doesn't ever make you laugh.

G.

Dear G,
No. When I think of people who make me laugh, it*s you. In person and in your writing.

Sofia

August 1, 2017

Dear Sofia,
You're carrying a heavy load. You now have within you Sandro's photo of his wife. So beside yourself you're now also carrying another woman on your back. That's even

more than I'm carrying. How can you manage such a big burden?

Simple. Just shake 'em off.

Giorgio

PS. That phrase you liked: kissing a girl through a thin silken kerchief. Actually, it's not mine. It's a famous image created by the great Hebrew writer, the national poet of Israel, Chaim Nachman Bialik.

*

August 1, 2017

Dear Giorgio,

Reading your email brought a smile on my face. Yes, joie de vivre is my best part. So let's put sadness aside.

Sometimes a word, or a call, an email it's enough to dismiss my sad feelings, to switch my mood...

I took a long nap by the swimming pool and I feel better.

Maybe in the future I will ask you the best way to find an editor, or maybe about self publishing. Maybe helping Aarvo with this is something is should do.

I know that the subject of the silkworm book it's not of interest for us. But I range from silkworm to bookworm (ha ha ha).

Write to me your words, your comments are so beneficent to me...

Another thing. I want to tell you is this:

Remember how when we met and I wanted to call you, out of respect, signor, and you said I should just call you Giorgio, but now, since my letters are going to be about *amore*, I hope you won't/don't mind if I call you by Mozart's favorite name, he loved the Italian version of Amadeus, Amadeo, since you have that same fun-loving sense of humor and straightforward fearless personality, remember how Mozart didn't shrink or hold back from telling the emperor, after the premier of his greatest opera, The Magic Flaute, when the emperor said to Mozart, as both he and the emperor were leaving the opera hall, "Too many notes, my dear Mozart, too many notes," Mozart wasn't afraid of replying at once with, "Just enough, Your Majesty, just enough."

I love, I am slowly eating up, devowring, your funny and touching love story of the Yemenite girl and of Professor Shultish infatuation with her. Whenever I have to stop reading, I mean I have to stop reading sometime and do other things, don't I?

I look forward to returning to La Ragazza Yemenita, like a child during a boring lunch yearning for the later ice cream desert. And I was and am so happy for you that this novel has come out in Italy.

I will do my best to put black on white emotions, feelings, images of my life. And I don't mind repeating what I wrote before. Because I keep thinking of those words: I'm very blessed to have crossed your path in Parma.

Yours,
Sofia

⁓

With Sandro at a cafe

Dear Amadeo,
No. Not the current husband.

Sofia

⁓

Dear Sofia,
So if it's not the current one, it must be the ex.

A.

⁓

August 2, 2017

Dear Sofia,
Amadeo is fine with me; I too love Mozart and still get
pangs in my heart when I remember he lived only 36 short
years.

Sofia loves my book and also the name Amadeo, a word that has, as Sofia put it, "love" built into it. And *I* love the way she pronounces my name, even though I don't hear it. I just see it. I look at the letters and between each one I imagine music, silently singing:

A♪ m a♪ d e♪♪ o♪

So many vowels give so many notes, and I sing them together with her, the vibrato of the "m" and the "d" as bridge between the neighboring vowels.

I hear the four-syllable Italian, low-pitched contralto of Sofia's voice as she writes her version of my name, no doubt say/singing it as she types it. So now it's Amadeo, which means "loves God" or "lover of God." But I'd rather have her feel AmaGiorgio.

Sofia writes "editor," ("you had to struggle to find an editor") but is referring to "editore," which in Italian means publisher. It is publisher Sofia wants to say.

When Sofia writes that the silkworm book "is not of interest for us," here again, for a moment, she is conjoining herself with me, separating our interests from that of Aarvo's. And she signs off with that evocative "Yours."

Again there is a possible Freudian lapse in the sentence, "helping Aarvo is something is should do..." What would a psychologist say about that "is" as a substitute for "I"? It's as though she is saying, without saying it, that someone else, something else, some "is," some third party, should help but not I.

I sense that a wonderful warmth has been created between Sofia and me. Now I feel ready to call her, chat, inquire how she is, and then ask her if she'd be willing to answer a question that buzzed through my head right after I saw her alluring face: how much she looked like that other Sophia, an image that keeps running in my mind like a little film. Film, flame (the one I think she gave me from her heart), almost same sound. Same basic letters.

August 3, 2017

Cara Sofia,

Thanks for writing from your vacation. I'm sure that after that nice long letter—getting it off your chest—you will
feel better. I know you will, because, as you say, your joie
de vivre is really the best part of you, not sadness.

No, as I said in that short email, I don't think I would
like to read that silkworm book. I don't read that sort of
stuff anyway, so I wouldn't be the best person to comment
on it.

Stay well, and let me hear you laugh all the way across
the ocean.

I will call you soon.

Best,
A

There's an apt Yiddish word for this namby-pamby letter. *Falsh.*
False. What a piece of crap. It says one thing but really means something else. But doesn't that reflect most people's false politesse conversation? Like "you're looking good." But regarding reading Aarvo's
unusual book, I was not *falsh.*

My phrase, "getting it off your chest." Soon as I wrote that, I at
once thought of her beautifully endowed chest, remembering her as
she stood before me on the Parma beach last month and took off that
light blue terrycloth robe and revealed that skimpy two-piece bathing

suit, the top of which held only one tiny part of those weighty, well-formed boobs that spilled over into the real world beyond their shiny orange cloth confines, which made her look more like Sophia L. than ever before. And I think of Sandro and Aarvo fondling, dandling, kissing, clasping or in any other way enjoying those luscious breasts, when I should be telling her that neither of them have any business going anywhere near them.

Which reminds me. I had thought of it all along, whom she resembled, but I didn't want to deflect from our initial conversation. I certainly didn't want that to be the centerpiece of our first meeting. But I will pursue it.

Who Sofia looks like.

As far as Sofia is concerned, I may be creating myself as a neuter, non-involved wise man. And where do I come up with that ridiculous phrase, "laugh all the way across the ocean"? Has she paralyzed my pen?

And with that in mind, I made my decision. I will call her and finally ask the question I have been wanting to ask.

I dialed Sofia's number in Parma, knowing that it's plus six hours there.

The phone was ringing and my heart was beating quicker with each ring, wondering what her reaction would be.

"Pronto," Sofia said cheerily, using the typical Italian phone greeting. First time I heard that word years ago, I thought of the American slang word for "quick"—so I thought "pronto" meant, "Hurry up and talk 'cause I'm busy." But I soon learned "pronto" means "Ready, I'm all ears." I.e., the Italian equivalent of "Hello."

"Hi," I said. "It's me."

"Amadeo!" Sofia's shriek of joy sent a thrill through me. She recognized my voice at once. "How are you?"

The way she uttered those three words was significant. They were three even sounds, without the American accent on the "are," which always sounded phony, forced, and falsely enthusiastic.

"Wonderful. Hope the same with you, Sofia with a "f". Glad I finally caught you at home."

She gave a delighted, musical laugh and said, "How nice that you're calling."

"So tell me, Sofia, how are things going?"

She knew what I meant. I didn't want to start at once with the real intent of my call, so I hinted at her situation.

"No real changes. By now you know my story."

"I do. And by now you know what I think."

"Of course I know from your penetrating letters."

"And?"

"And what?" Sofia asked.

"Are you doing anything about it?"

Silence. Silence too was an answer. She didn't say yes, she didn't say no. Sofia was stuck.

"Listen, dear Sofia, since I have you on the phone, I have a question for you. Sofia, I've known you for a while and there's something I always wanted to ask you but never did."

"For you, dear Amadeo, anything. Ask anything you like."

There was a subdued lover's vibrato in her voice, intimate, embracing, wide open like a gate.

"That's so sweet of you, Sofia. Typical of your usual geniality. Okay. Here it is. From the first moment—well maybe not the first moment, because the first moment I saw you I wasn't aware of it, but soon thereafter—what I'm going to say now, the thought that has been hovering in me, has been bubbling on my lips and I didn't utter it because I didn't want it to distract from our conversation, from my relationship with you. But I'm sure you have been asked this question before."

Again silence.

I thought we were cut off.

"Hello? Hello! Sofia!"

"Yes, I'm here." The tone now slightly different, the three words as if through pursed lips.

I guess she knew what was coming. So I said it: "You know what I'm going to say."

Again she didn't reply. I spoke but didn't want to speak. I started, then changed my mind. Thinking it's not worth breaking up this beautiful friendship just for that bit of info that I intuited anyway. But I couldn't take back what I had begun. Sometimes a person can get a grip on the words he senses he shouldn't say and can overcome the desire to say them. But there are times when the words you realize you shouldn't say come out anyway because you feel that if you don't say them now, you might never say them. So my words went flying. No way out. It was like trying to withdraw a letter you've just mailed from one of those big, round, blue mailboxes.

"Soon as I saw those lovely, those stunning sloe eyes of yours, your nose and the flare of those beautifully cut nostrils, and your full lips, it struck me. And especially combined with your name. You've been asked this before, right?"

I thought I would get silence again, but Sofia said, "Right." Quietly. As if purposely subduing her acquiescence. Yes, she did look like that other Sophia, with a "ph," but my Sofia was no clone. Her slightly wider, fuller jaw and her nose, just a wee bit thicker at the nostrils, that she no doubt got from her father, whoever he was. Who it was I wasn't going to ask. If she volunteered, fine; if not, I would remain discreetly silent. But these two, I'm not going to call them flaws, let's just say differences, in no way diminished from her attractiveness, her pretty, yes, sexy face, especially those lookalike sloe eyes and full lips. Oh, those eyes of hers, those green eyes of Sofia's. And Sophia's. Those eyes pulled. For nothing's more alive than eyes, and in hers life's breath pulsed. And so did words, in alphabets of tongues unknown. Desire lay languid in those eyes, but wariness too. The parted lips concealed other promises.

"And how do you respond?" I asked, the image of the other Sophia filling my mind's eye.

"When this question is asked, I don't say much," Sofia replied. "I sort of shrug and say, just a coincidence. Or some variation. And by the cool expression on my face, the other person if he's smart, and they usually are, learns to be quiet. Not to pursue it."

I knew I should have stopped. For I already got my answer. But I wanted more. We always want more. The demon in me made me persist, even though I feared she might lose patience or even hang up.

"But since I don't see the expression on your face, I *am* going to pursue it, especially since you told me to ask anything I like."

Silence once more. That's it, I thought. Finito. Now I overstepped my bounds.

For a moment I felt a curtain had fallen.

Then, bless her, came low-pitched words, shining with a soft glow of their own, the tone not related at all to their meaning, a glow that lifted me up from the gloom of my own creation.

"But for you, dear Amadeo—"

Soon as I heard those words my life stuff returned. I hovered. I rose. I flew.

"—since you have been so kind, so helpful, so generous with me, I will tell you. And you will be the first person aside from my husband to who I have revealed this. Yes..." and she hesitated a moment, and I felt I was at the birth of something momentous, "yes, I am...we are... but severed from her fame."

I liked that word "severed." Even though she pronounced it "severe."

Still she did not confirm. She did not go into the relationship, but I gathered from her words, her unsaid words, words I had been privileged to hear.

"You see, I have always been independent and always wanted to make my own way. So I didn't even take on her family name. I assumed a variation of her original name and made it Rallazzo. No one saw the connection. And when people looked at my eyes and lips and the rest of me and made a comment I just waved my hand, made a face and said, *I wish*. Believe it or not, *that* and not so much the wave of hand or puzzled, questioning look or twisted, astonished, disparaging, is that the right word?"

I nodded, then laughed. How can she hear my nod?

"Yes, that's the word."

"Yes, a disparaging face. But, as I said, you know what was the clinch? The words '*I wish*'—that was the clinch."

"And schooling?"

"Yes, of course. I went to college, incognito, and studied on my own."

"But wasn't a way of life all set for you? Weren't you ever tempted to go into show business?"

"Never. I didn't want, had no desire, for that way of life at all. And, anyway, I was shy, withdrawn. And I always made my own way financially."

"Do you see her?"

"Once in a while."

The flat, reserved timbre of those last four words, they also clued me not to go into familial relationships.

"Thank you, dear Sofia, thank you so much for confiding in me. I feel so privileged. Thank you. And I give you the same loving hug I gave you when we first met. But even warmer and huggier."

And then returned the familiar upbeat tone, as though she had switched personality.

She laughed and said, "Yes, I remember that embrace."

"I remember it too."

"I'm so glad you called, Amadeo. So wonderful to hear your voice."

"Yours too. Your voice is like music. Mozart's."

"You are a darling, Amadeo. I can't tell you that enough."

"Just keep saying it. Practise."

I heard a delicious laugh, then Sofia had to say goodbye because she was off for an appointment.

I did it. Took a chance. Might have lost her. But she was so genial and, yes, loving, that at the end I felt her warmth even more.

During our phone talk, you notice, not a word about her puzzling cafe scenario with Sandro.

And the following morning I got this fascinating, as you will see, "fellow up" letter from her:

With Sandro in a cafe

Dear Amadeo,
Wrong.

S.

Dear Sofia,
So if it's not the current one, not the ex, which one is it? It doesn't make sense.

Unless it's the future one. So what's the correct answer?

Amadeo

With Sandro in the cafe

Dear Amadeo,

Let me continue the narrative.

Luckily, it's a summer day and Sandro was wearing this wide big straw hat to protect his head from the sun. The hat is on the chair next to me. I quickly take the hat, put it on my head and drape the brim down way over my face, and I bend my head down so I shouldn't be seen. Sandro asks me why I'm doing this and I whisper, "The sun is in my eyes." And he believes me.

But, luckily, _____, who is probably looking for a table and sees all are taken, leaves the cafe.

Sofia

August 3, 2017

Caro Amadeo,   A PS to our phone chat

So wonderful talking to you. I want to add a few fellow up words to our conversation of yesterday.

You know, my mother originally spelled her first name just the way I do now, but then either Ponti or De Sica suggests she change the spelling to "ph," perhaps because Americans are used to that spelling.

And did you know her family name was Scicolone? It almost sounds like an Italian version of the American word "cyclone," and that when Sophia was a kid, other kids gave her a knickname, "stuzzicadenti"—toothpick, because she was so scrawny.

That Italian word is so fascinating and so fitting for her because "stuzzi" means "appetizing" and the verb "stuzzicare" means "to tease," both words which you can so well associate with her.

I also want to tell you, despite what you may see on Internet, she never, never ever, never posed naked. **Never.** All those nude photos you see of her are faked. They get someone with a similar build to pose naked and then with trick photography and clever printing they carefully fuse her face onto someone else's naked body.

All best,
Sofia, with an "f"

August 3, 2017

Caro Amadeo,
I finished finally last night your romanza, *La Ragazza Yemenita*, with the complete version of Shultish's translation of the old writer's famous story. What an ending!

You have terrific insites, Giorgio, into your characters souls and inner essence.

Regarding me. Very exciting details coming. Very soon. Next email.

Yesterday was a turbulent day here and I will share it
with you in my next letter.

Abbracc,
Sofia

Now, with Sofia having read my novel, a new dimension has come
into our half epistolary, half personal, and fully human relationship.

In addition to her mostly Finn, partly Swedish (and who knows
how many other infinitesimal Nordic parts?) husband Aarvo and her
boyfriend Sandro, I have come into the equation, a presumably neutral, objective ear, the only part of me that, vis-à-vis Sofia, is objective
and neutral.

But Sofia still doesn't know about the "presumably." Yet. But that
neutral disguise will eventually be stripped away.

Now there's four of us—excluding boyfriend Sandro's shadowy,
as-yet-unnamed, wife, whom we know only from a photo Sandro took.

What attracted me to Sofia? Her looks? Her allure? Well, it began
soon as I saw her at the Parma beach. And I guess her being in love
with a guy who would never give her the full-time attention she needed
and deserved played a role too. It enhanced the dream. Because she was
a challenge? Because of whom she looked like? Because she loved my
novel? One of the above. Some of the above. All of the above.

About me Sofia knew little. She knew I was a writer. But she never
asked about my personal life, my past, my education. Seems to me she
assumed I was not married, and on that score she was right. She even
liked, and told me she loved, my curiosity. She knew I was a bit older
than her but never asked my age or if I had parents, brothers, sisters.
But she did surprise me once, asking me when my birthday was. Maybe
her awe of me as a writer re- or suppressed any natural inclination to ask
questions. She never even asked where I lived. She assumed near New

York because that's where everyone lived. Some people, like Sofia, are more confiding than curious. Me I'm just the opposite. In me people confide, but it was never a two-way street. Most people soon forget personal details anyway, or they become fuzzed in one's brain. So it's better to be tight-lipped. You never know what misinformation people spread.

"Turbulent"—never saw her use that word before. Again keeping me in suspense until the morrow.

With Sandro in the cafe

Dear Amadeo,
Here's the correct answer. It was in my first letter. This scene could also be in a movie. You see, it's an imagined movie. I guess it's my fear of being discovered. If I had seen Aarvo come into a cafe where I'm sitting with Sandro, I would of froze. Not know what to do. I don't think I would have the wit to snatch Sandro's hat and hide behind it.

I hope you enjoyed my little made-up movie.

Sofia

PS Another version could be this: I sit in a cafe with Sandro. Because it's a cloudy day he carries an umbrella. Suddenly, he opens the umbrella. And I say, "But it's not raining." "Gotta run," he says. And I understand right away. He has probably seen his wife, and he later confirms this. He had thought she was at home in his town, not in Parma. And I didn't even see her. Because of the open black umbrella.

With Sandro at a cafe

Dear Sofia,
What a marvelous, suspenseful scenario you created.

Brava,
Amadeo

August 3, 2017

Dear Amadeo,
Thank you. Now back to reality. And what reality.
Still in France, family vacation. Sounds so homey and natural.
But wait.
Fireworks coming. What I hinted at in my previous email.
Soon you will feel the surprise I felt today.
Listen. And this is no movie. This is all too real.
I wake up. It's 9:30 and the apartment is silent. I check my little Neemi's room and he is sleeping. I walk around, no sign of Aarvo.

Then I check my phone and there I see two messages from him.

From the beach.

One is called "loyalty" the other one "your mail." I feel like a punch in the stomach. I don't know which one to read first. Then decide and open "your mail."

Turns out that I forgot and left my gmail open on my computer and Aarvo has been reading my correspondence...and he has questions for me.

Forgetting and leaving your email open can only happen in a post-modern electronic age, where everything is saved on a phone or a computer, while old-fashioned letters are sent via post (remember that old method of communicating? Now it's called snail mail) and locked into a private desk drawer. But Freudians—they seem to be all over the place in Sofia's letters—would contend there's no such thing as forgetting. I'm no Freudian but re Sofia I would agree with them. What she did was done purposely. Intentionally. With subconscious planning aforethought. She, who denies Sandro is machiavelic, is being machiavelic herself. She *wanted* Aarvo to discover this romanza so as to put an end to her, their, tenuous, unsatisfying relationship. As Sofia wrote: screwed the first marriage, and if I could would probably also do it with the second.

But here too I don't know if I can, or will, share these thoughts with her. Who knows? Aarvo may read this too. I'll suggest to her that she get another email, one just for her phone. Now seeing her words, the shock of them, the novelistic surprise of them, I also feel I was punch in the stomach.

Soon as I saw those lines, that dramatic turn in her life, I could see it, so cinematic it was, I cried out, "Oh, no!"

In the olden days, lovers would use a post office box for secret communication.

And then I continue to read what Sofia has written. She has come to the same conclusion about Freud. Amazing how we think alike. But if I were pressed, like she's being pressed by the Finn, what explanation would I give? That I'm writing a story?

And I think, and likely Sofia does too, that luckily Aarvo did this confrontation via email and not in person. Because this way it gives her time to think, plan, consider various responses.

First Aarvo asks, why do I share intimate thoughts with you? Secondly who is Sandro?

What would I do if I were caught like that? Perhaps pressure forces you to come up with a plausible response: He's my fantasy of you. Or, my girlfriend, knowing I'm interested in writing, wants me to write up her story, but felt it would be more authentic-sounding if I wrote it in the first person. And I'm getting advice from a fiction writer.

Would I believe that if I were Aarvo? Not for a moment.

My heart stops beating. For a second or more. My God, what do I do now?

I walk in circles and my head is exploding. Shit. How could I forget gmail open?? I'm so mad at myself. I don't think of Freudian's "atto mancato," hoping to be caught.

Which actually means: failure to act. So we're linked again with both of us thinking of Freud. Coming to exactly the same conclusion: hoping to be caught, by not acting with care. Which I get to by thinking about it, while she gets to it ass-backwards by *not* thinking about it.

Oh I'm so mad. At, with, myself. Then I feel violated. My privacy, my secret garden is been violated. I'm furious. I want to scream.

My all body is in sweat. I need to go to the toilet. Then I take a shower. To cool down. And think. I start breathing. Again. Finally.

Now I feel violated too. As if *I've* been caught.

Oxygen gets in my veins and slowly to my brain. I have to make up my mind fast. What shall I say? Shall I take this opportunity to tell the truth?

Yes. Do it. Finally. I send Sofia a silent command. Isn't it time to make the break? When I write this word I think of its homonym: brake. Put finally the brake on your phony chugging together.

There are so many wonderful puns I could play with. I recall Aarvo's nationality. He's Finnish, so maybe it's time Sofia is finish with him. It's already built into his personhood. Just turn adjective to verb. All she has to do is act. Finish. Maybe with him and with Sandro too.

Maybe.

But one second after I know that I won't do it. Won't tell the truth. I don't know if it's cowardice. No. I'm not a coward. Sandro told me about our wings.

Remember? And also letting* Sandro out of this story... there are mechanisms...and there is Neemi...

*either a typo for getting—or she means leaving him out of the story.

So I call Aarvo.

☙

Dear Sofia,
Again I have to write you in middle of reading your letter.

How lucky you are that this was done via email and written messages. Can you imagine your reaction had the Finn confronted you in person? Truth is, when I read you were caught, I was so terror-stricken, petrified, stomach-punched, at you being caught,

I thought Aarvo had confronted you in person, and only a bit later did I realize that this happened via email and that there was a miraculous distance between both of you, and I breathe easy, sigh with relief.

Amadeo

☙

(Sofia's letter, continued:)

Aarvo is still on the beach. I tell him about the emails.

And tell him something that it's true. I'm sending you, Amadeo, some writings...some drafts of something that could become a novel or not. It's fiction. And you are my mentor. You take your time and read my few sentences. I tell Aarvo that I did not share this with him because he is busy with his work and I did not want to disturb him. I did not forget to shut down my email because there is nothing to hide. And Sandro is an old friend. I share some lines with him, because he is also good with writing.

Reading this, I think: brilliant idea, well thought out. Same thing I thought of independently. A fiction.

But I hear in Aarvo's voice that he is not totally convinced. He read the word "love" somewhere and he is not stupid. So I tell him I'm trying some sentences. The sound of words. And there is some truth in all I'm saying. I believe my words. I hope he does too....

I just don't want Aarvo to pronounce Sandro's name. Aarvo's questions where is Sandro from just don't find an answer. I ask Aarvo to concentrate on his book, on constructive thoughts and not to freak out* of misunderstanding.

*I think the word "because" should be inserted after "freak out."

Still, all day I have this feeling of being at his mercy. He will probably come back with questions that will not find answers. I just wish Aarvo never saw Sandro's name. Because that name is mine. And mine only.

Still need time to digest all this...

Hope you are well, dear dear Amadeo. Apparently laugh is not behind* the corner for me just yet...but these are interesting** days here in France.

It's all very Almodovar***, without the gayish**** mother...

Ciaoooooo

S.

*for "behind" read "around." She's surely translating from the Italian.

**what a wasted, empty word. What's so "interesting" about her situation? It's not interesting. It's upsetting. Unsettling. Awful. Suspenseful. Gut-wrenching. A person, a book, can be interesting. But not that scene.

***Boy, Sofia sure is bright and on the ball. She is referring to Pedro Almodovar, the director of the epic Spanish film, *All About My Mother*, where there is a fluidity of sexual orientations and other personality changes. One character says something like, "You become more authentic the more you resemble what you have dreamed of becoming." Certainly a very apropos reference.

****For a moment I read the word "gayish" as "goyish," but then realized that the very goyish italiana Sofia couldn't possibly know that Yiddish adjective which means "gentile."

August 5, 2017

Amadeo, caro,
I hope this email finds you well.
Couple of days ago I have sent you two emails but did not hear from you.
One was named "A like Amore" and the other one "Yesterday." I wrote them from my berry using a new server or whatever you call it in computer language, so I was wondering if my mails made it to you or they are wandering in the internet void??
Here it's all well. Things are calm and I'm enjoying some sun and swimming.

Ciao, hope to read you soon,
Sofia

Well, things must have quieted down. She writes no more about jealous Aarvo's questions. Apparently, he believed her, the Finnish fool.

But what an abrupt change of tone from one day to another. I'm actually as shocked as she was when she got that email from her husband on the beach. The other day she was almost ruined. At wit's end. Didn't know what to do.

Today, enjoying the beach. Calm and cool, warm and sunny. Something's screwy here.

August 5, 2017

Cara Sofia,

I did **not** get either of those two tantalizingly named emails. As you surely know, I only got that stunning one, so dramatic, like out of a film or a play, where you describe how Aarvo emails you from the beach after discovering and reading your private emails and how cleverly you responded.

Since in your current email I see no turmoil, no aftershocks from the other day's quake, I presume the Finn believed you and all has quieted down after this near disaster. What a change!

All best,
Amadeo

Now comes another turn in her story so incredible, it's like out of a dream. Or a fantasy novel. I couldn't believe it. Like that little marble-shaped flame that Sofia either gave—or didn't give—me from her heart when we parted by the beach in Parma a few weeks ago.

Just like I was stunned that she wanted me to be an ear for her affair, I was now stunned and surprised by another turn in her love story.

How? Listen to this. I search for one of Sofia's earlier emails to make sure I have correctly transcribed her English and that I have not overly corrected her occasionally flawed, but charmingly flawed, English. And this is in combination with wondering why in one of her last letters to me she had written,

I decided to tell my story starting 2 years ago in 2015 when I have found Sandro again, after 9 years of silence.

Of not being in touch for 9 long years. From then I will continue my story. Of course, I will also write about now, 2017,
in Parma. But you will see it is not in chronological order.

but then Sofia doesn't say anything, not a word, about the long ago. I
figured she decided not to include any of this past history and backed
off from revealing some intimate details. It always intrigued me, these
details about the past, how a romance was rekindled.

Just then I made an important discovery which will soon be revealed. Sofia had attached something to an email and I had completely
overlooked that tiny paper clip, the computer screen's signal for an
attachment.

Absolutely fantastic. Coming in a minute. After my own justified
plaint.

By now I had already settled into my new job. Me, a consultant.
Almost full time. Hardly any time for creating. I couldn't believe it.
Given Sofia's flirtatiousness when we met at the Parma beach—remember how she stood up from being stretched out on that canvas lounge
chair, wrapped in a pale blue terrycloth robe and, while standing before
me, unbound herself from that robe and revealed her skimpy two-piece
orange bikini, showing me that tanned, shapely body that so much
reminded me of that other Sophia?—I could have sworn, and anyone
else looking, watching, observing, would have sworn too, that she was
interested in me, and not only interested but dying to make an impression. Why the Italian Air Force helicopter flying overhead didn't swoop
down and scoop her up, I'll never understand.

How could I forget her stance, the tone of her voice, her gestures?
The dancing light in her eyes. The shifting musical scale of her smile.
The happy n ♪ o ♪ t ♪ e ♪ s of her words.

I'm also very good at reading, analyzing, interpreting decorated
silence, movements that have unsaid words woven into them.

And now I'm into this.

Advising. Sympathizing. Commenting. What a journey! Put on a slowly crawling freight train from Romanticism to Platonism. Or is it Platonicism? And with a one-way ticket, no less.

Don't get me wrong. I admired Plato (that's Plato, not Pluto), and was always jealous that he had a teacher I could never have. If pressed to the wall I'd even compose verses in Plato's honor.

But the neuter, just-friendship movement connected with his name was not for me. What a neuter remark: not for me. You see, neuterism is catching. An insidious, invidious virus. What I really wanted to say is: abhorrent.

I abhor platonicism. Platonicism for me is like imposing vegetarianism on a carnivore or abstinence on a lover of liquor. Reminds me of the old Yiddish saying: A platonic is a Potatonik without kick. Others say: without a click.

Despite me being taken on as Sofia's apprentice advisor, still, still, nevertheless, I was able to tease out of all her letters an understone

(I'm also good at reading undertones) of affection.

Wait a minute. I wrote "understone," another one of those stupid but meaningful typos. Affection between us has been swooshed under a stone.

Affection has gradations, I know. And it also depends on Sofia's intent, what meaning she was putting into those words to me. All those double dears, those kisses and embraces at the end of her letters, plus the "I want to see you again," could not possibly be totally platonic. Perhaps Sofia intended them as brotherly-sisterly friendly, but her subconscious added, or shifted to, elided toward, another meaning. Like "Yours, Sofia." Whose is she? Not Aarvo's. Not Sandro's.

It was as if she were writing two languages at once. The very same letters with two different meanings. Like the Korean and Chinese alphabets. Same alphabet, different vocabulary. In one sentence the same twelve characters or pictograms that meant in Korean "an elephant is in your knapsack," might mean in Chinese, "the old widow was un-knit-ting an obstinate onion."

On the surface, Sofia's kisses at the end of the letters were *baci* on the cheeks. But if you peeled away some of the politesse, the innate warmth of the ligatures rose, breathed, escaped, and the kiss on the cheeks slid sideways to become a kiss on the lips.

Now we'll get to those intriguing details about the Sofia-Sandro romanza that Sofia had attached in an email I had completely over-looked.

As I said, a little "paper clip" logo was attached to that email. Now, after several weeks of email exchanges, I click on that recently discov-ered "paper clip" and open up her attached letter. And there before me is the long and detailed answer to my puzzlement about the beginning of the affair, and the confirmation that indeed Sofia was absolutely right when she says she will tell her story "starting two years ago," but in the body of the email she didn't tell me that this story was attached. She depended on my skill with a computer to notice that little paper clip logo or icon.

And so a bit of serendipity now opened up for me a new chapter of Sofia's past. She begins by detailing, in writerly depth and in paint-erly colors, and with a passion I had not seen until now, her feelings at re-meeting Sandro after an absence of nine years.

I breath irregularly, or maybe I don't breath at all. My all body shivers even if outside the temperature is above 35 degrees Celsius. My head turns and my thoughts are frozen or spinning like crazy molecules. Tomorrow I have an appointment.

With Sandro. I have dreamed about this moment for nine years. How can the heart bear this without bursting? Some days I even thought that I might not see him again.

Ever. Just the very thought of not seeing him, even once, scared me to death. Impossible. Somehow, somewhere, I had to meet him again.

Destiny decided that it would be tomorrow.

It's impossible for me to stay still. I wish I could scream to the entire world that

I will meet him again. But I can't. My little boy Neemi is playing in the swimming pool and he should have an attentive mom, but I cannot help and let my thoughts wonder away. When was the last time I had seen Sandro?? I knew it perfectly. June 20, 2008. Nine years without seeing or having news of Sandro. More than nine long long years....

I try to explain to Viviana, my oldest friend since childhood, she lived next door, who will accompany me tomorrow, how I feel. Impossible or maybe sounds impossible, but Viviana knows me since I was 6 yrs old and she know how to follow my hectic way of speaking and thinking.

We are spending our summer vacation together in Sicily with our families. Pure coincidence. But coincidence, just read all the novels, is the real, the ultimate reality. Anyway, we, that is, each of us, me with my family, Sandro with his, invent an excursion. Just the two of us. We will leave our kids with a parent and we take the day off.

I tell Viviana that I just want to see him once. I need to see him one more time. But as I say this I know I'm lying. Not to Viviana. To myself. I wonder if she sees through this. She probably does. She knows me well enough. Senses my deep feelings for Sandro. I know that every time I meet him I totally lose control. But still I lie....

I want to see him. I desire it. Totally. Completely.

This night seems endless but somehow I fall asleep

and I dream of Sandro.

I dream we are walking hand in hand. But we are not walking on ground. We float 2-3 feet above the earth. Levitating.

The next day I'm so excited. Pure energy. The heat in Palermo is unbearable but I don't care. I slowly get ready, prepare myself to this encounter. Viviana gives some advices on how to dress, to comb my hair. She takes part of the ceremony. I feel like a bride. But no family member leads me. I'm overwhelmed by emotions. We get in the car. Viviana sits beside me and after having said goodbye to the kids, hers and mine, we leave for this journey. Driving to the outskirts of Palermo to go and meet Sandro.

I enjoy every turn, curve. I enjoy the anticipation of this moment. Roads are beautiful and I smile at the beauty of this landscape. I feel alive.

A road sign shows that the little town of Castello is not far away. I try to control all my senses. It's hot and I'm sweating. My hair is getting fuzzy and my shirt is soaking wet.

I arrive in Castello. Have to find a parking place.

Done.

Have to find the square.

Done.

Have to find Sandro. My eyes are scanning the square. I see people. Stores. But where is he? My mouth is dry. My heart is beating furiously. I want to see him.

Now. Adesso.

Then behind a pillar I see a guy smiling at me.

It's Sandro.

I have found him. I don't think anymore. I run toward him. He opens his arms and hugs me.

I'm home again.

I don't even say Done. Because Done shows something completed. Finished. Done. But this is just beginning.

Viviana, she doesn't know what to say. We are still hugging. I don't want to let Sandro go. Maybe I'm just dreaming, so I want to linger in this dream a little longer. Then slowly we let this embrace go and I introduce Viviana to Sandro. We drink something in a bar. To break the ice and to quench our thirst. Everything seems normal and surreal at the same time. It's like a movie in slow motion... sounds are muffled, colors are sepia. My heart keeps on racing. Sandro asks me to follow him. We leave Viviana on the heated square, promising her to be back a little hour later. Sandro leads me to his car and I let him take me away...in all senses.

I cannot tell you how I feel, maybe a novelist or a song writer can finds words for this...I can't. I only know that I want this sensation of joy, happiness, thrill, ecstasy, golden dream, to last forever.

I know it's hot, but I throw it away like an unwanted cap.

Then finally the second physical contact. He touches my knee while he drives, and that touch goes up and down my leg, up and down my body.

About ten minutes later we get to this small village. The view is magnificent. We park and we walk around this old place. I talk and talk. Fast. I don't take breaks. I want to stop time. I want to hear his voice. I want to hug him and tell him that I love him. Simply like that but I can't. I'm afraid of looking in his eyes. But I get glimpse of him. He is beautiful. His lips, eyes, smile. I need to touch him. But he precedes me. He grabs me and he pulls me towards him. He kisses me. I don't know if it's the heat or the emotion but I hear my heart pumping in my ears. This is what I call happiness.

Pure joy. Is there a better word for ecstasy?

I know we as humans have words. Language. Symbols of various kinds joined together to express thoughts. But for what I feel this moment there are no words, letters or signs. The thought, the feelings, they run through me. I have no words for them.

Feeling his lips on mine. Again. I'm dizzy. My all body wants him badly. I desire him. Totally. I try to tell him how I feel but I don't need to find words. He also feels the same way. We did not see each other for 9 years but now, together, it is like picking up a dialog never interrupted. I'm in total symbiosis with him...we are perfect.

But now I have to turn clock back to how it happened. How we found each other.

Two months before, in mid June, I received a message that Sandro had accepted my friendship on Facebook. I had been searching for him for so long. Knew his address in a town near Parma, but once when I tried to call him, a woman replied to the phone and I heard a baby crying so I hang up the phone. Feeling miserable. How could I join to him? How send him a message? I had searched all internet engines to find information of Sandro. I had found out that he was a star ping pong player.

Unbelievable, what you can find on internet. Scary how every body knows everything about every body else. I had made up a plan to connect to a ping pong organization, asking them to give Sandro my email address. Then froze by the fear of never getting a reply from them. Also, my fear of not knowing if he would get the message and then decide not to reply, or maybe never get the message at all. Decided that all these plus possible rejection was too much to bear.

And so I gave up my plan. But never stopped thinking of him. I had already checked Facebook. Several times. Some Sandro were listed but no one seemed to match my guy. Till one day in May when I saw a photo. This can be Sandro I told myself. Hair is gone, but I recognize his smile. Was it possible to lose so much hair in 9 years? I send him a message:

I don't know if you are the right Sandro, but if the book by Boccaccio rings a bell it means you are the right person!

Two nights later, FB sent his acceptance.

How to describe how I felt? Probably the same way people feel when they find a treasure they thought lost forever.

The next day I got an email from Sandro, which I was, am, so excited I share with you.

This is exactly his email. I just re-copy it.

NOOO ! ! ! ! ! I don't believe this!!!
This isn't really possible.
Someone pinch me, please!
How are you?
What are you doing?
And where are you? dove sei?
And with whom are you?

But mostly, how are you?

I don't dare to think how your life has changed, even what do you see outside your window.

(Giorgio, I am commenting on that last phrase of Sandro. I did not understand it. But I'm so excited reading, hearing his words, it doesn't bother me.)

I'm always the same, or better. I delude myself, also because it seems to me that since last time I saw you just one year has passed, but in reality I can't even make the calculation. However, I am fine. I have a beautiful set of twins, girls, and this is the real, the ultimate truth. So for now I say goodbye and I give you a great big hug.

Sandro

And I reply to Sandro with a long long email.

Amadeo, I have translated for you my first reply letter to Sandro below, all of it.

If you don't have the time or interest in reading it, and believe me, I can't blame you, I have used a different font for it. So, if you wish, you can skip it.

Yeah, sure, I'm gonna skip this exciting email!

So then, here, below, is the translation of my letter to Sandro:

You can not even imagine my joy...!!

I've been looking for a lot of information about you

*on internet for years (like your table tennis results!) And
I've thought several times to send a message to the table
tennis organization, but then I thought, suppose my letter
never gets to you. I tried several times on FB and apart
from a strange Dali-like photo, I could not identify you...
until last night!*

I saw the pictures of your twins, they are beautiful! Really!

*I have a blonde little boy named Neemi who is 5 years
old! It is my great joy and my source of energy and stability.*

Deep inside of Sofia there›s always that little flame. I
do not know where to start since the last 9 years are not
easy to sum up ...*

* As I read this letter, again I feel the warm glow of that little
marble-sized fireball. It becomes more and more of a mystery, even as I
wonder if this really happened or if I dreamt it so vividly I assumed it
was real. But whether it happened or not, what is most real and most
important for me is that in my mind's eye I see how she went with her
hand to her heart and from there plucked that warm little flame that
she gave me.

Most overwhelming for me, however, is how much she's attached
to and loves Sandro. None of her previous letters even approaches this
narrative of hers.

So let's start ... ok?

*I've been married for 8 years with Aarvo, who is Finn-
ish (from Helsinki). Where else? I never heard of any other
city in Finland besides it. We met in London by chance
when I was vacationing there ... Like I told you, he has
been in silkworm eggs business for years, traveling a lot,*

especially to Japan to buy the tiny eggs of the silkworms, and after a short relationship (not with silkworms) I went to live in Finland.

After the Finland there was a short stay in Italy, in fact Neemi was born here in Parma, then again Aarvo's travels to Persia and to Japan. Marital life is not always easy, but children they help to make firm relationships and we rely on them to make easier the homework of life. Of course, paying taxes and sharing heavy weights is not easy...but it's part of the game!

But I have a small magic "secret garden"...that's enough for me!

A garden made up of some letters, cherishing the Boccaccio book that you gave me, and beautiful memories that warmed my heart in my hardest moments.

Sometimes a little magic is good...!

It will be 9 years but you've always been part of my thoughts, sometimes in the supermarket, sometimes while reading your gift book...in short, far be it from me to mess up our lives, but you always were part of mine. I hope that my words do not seem too risky and too bold, but I wanted after all these years to share with you this little secret.

A huge hug

Sofia

Of course I'm waiting for all your stories!

Yes, the book he gave me was the famous collection, *Decameron* by Boccaccio.

I click "SEND" and let my love for Sandro fly out via the web.

I wait for a reply.

Nothing.

Total silence.

One day. Two days.

Nothing.

Oh, my God, what have I done? Why did I tell him all this?? I should have waited. Thousand of "if" "what" "why" are attacking me from all over. But I had to tell him.

Punto.

Now listen to this. A couple of days later I get an email. It begins with:

"Knock, knock?? Where are you?? Did you get my letter from a few days ago?"

Now I get it. Now it hits me. Now I understand his silence.

He never got my email, it simply got lost! But where? Who knows? He asks me to send it again. And so I click SEND again. Without changing a word of my text. And this time I have no hesitations, no qualms. I am glad to let him know exactly how I feel, felt.

The reply arrives fast. He never had imagined that he meant so much for me. He too had thought of me during all this years, but never dared to contact me...We start to write to each other. We have 9 years to catch up. We want to know it all...One email, two, three...hundred of emails before this encounter in Sicily.

With husband Aarvo in silkworm business, that stunning silk scarf Sofia was wearing that first day I met her at the Parma beach suddenly makes sense. Now it hits me. Only fitting. Husband in silkworm trade gets for his wife a beautiful, light as a cloud, multicolored silk scarf made of his own silk that has a magical bird-like life of its own and ripples away in the mouth of a gull.

⟨℘⟩

August 9, 2017

Dear A,
Your *La Ragazza Yemenita* shows me how creativity
adds to life. You are so full of life and energy: a real source
of inspiration for me.
    Enjoy your trips, your work. I'm just a click away...write
to me when you can. I will start writing about my story
again soon.

    Take care.
    Sofia

Soon as I saw that polite, miles-away "take care" and not her more
personal "yours" a chill came over me—not "came over," rather, a cold
wave assaulted me. And it put an icy film over my affection for Sofia. I
didn't choose to do this. It's just what happened. My instinct told me
that with that "take care" she didn't really care. I was frosted from heart
to toe. Strange, what two words, two syllables, four letters each can do!
    Nevertheless, just like she doesn't let Sandro know the absolute
truth of her reactions to him, so I too suppress my disappointment and
I write her a *falsh*, cheery letter. Maybe I better speed up my plans of
going to Parma to see her. A trip I'd been thinking of for a while. Don't
be a Sofia, I say. Don't procrastinate.

⟨℘⟩

Aug. 9, 2017

Dear Sofia,
You are right. Been away. Back for a day and on my way again. Overloaded with journalistic work, so it will be a few days before I can reply. Please understand.

But I love getting letters from you. Your personality always shines through in your words. It feels like you're there in person.

Which is best of all. I like to be in touch with you.

Best,
A

Even if I have nothing to say I want to let her know it's great to be in touch with her.

Touch, what a multi-dimensional word. Remove the "be in" and the "with" and you have truth pulsing behind all the polite, reined-in platitudes.

August 15, 2017

Dear Amadeo,
Yes, I'm back home since yesterday. Vacation, finito.

Half of me is here, half there. It's like I'm split in 2, existing in some moderniste novel.

It's still very warm here in Parma and I actually have

the feeling I'm still on vacation...

I still keep thinking about the heroes of your book, Shultish, who keeps dreaming, and Bar Nun, who likes Shultish, but sort of toys with him.

I'm still amazed that the words I write in a book can entrance readers, make them become deeply involved with an entirely new group of people who have made an indelible impression on them, and whom these readers think of constantly. Living souls, with names, faces, memorable personalities, and experiences. Even to the extent that these readers want to intervene and make changes on the printed page to offer a character a more satisfying life. They consider those characters so real they want to breathe their own life into them.

One question: when you started writing did you already think about the ending??

I wrote back to her that I did not plan the ending as I began writing *The Yemenite Girl.*

(Sofia's letter, continued:)

I have read another romanza and I see the Casanova pattern...the idea of being in love, of being on the hunt more than actually loving a person...

In your book, are you Shultish the professor, or Bar Nun, the great Israeli writer.

OK, now I am switching from love books to love news...

Amazing how long this letter has gone on without mentioning her love problems.

> On the last week of August I will spend two days with Sandro. I'm so looking forward to it...we will probably go to Sicily...and have all the time in the world...

But she doesn't write how she can arrange this. Is her husband going away?

Who will take care of her little Neemi? How is Sandro arranging this with his wife?

> After my bad discussion with Sandro (remember the one at the restaurant), I have the feeling that we are more close...and more in love...
> Many more stories to come soon your way...
>
> Hugs,
> Sofia

There's something loony in Sofia's love affair, and I think Sofia is the loony one. How can she be possibly more close and more in love with him after all the complaints she has cited?

In one line "more in love"—with Sandro. In almost the next— hugs for me. These have to be platonic hugs and I don't like them.

15 agosto 2017

RE: who is who
Dear Sofia,
I hope you are well.

I am all the characters in *La Ragazza Yemenita*, even the waves of the sea. I'm also the camera recording everything. And all the periods and commas too.

Which falls into line re: Flaubert's famous remark about his novel, *Madame Bovary*, when he said he was all the characters, even Madame Bovary's cat.

By saying that Flaubert meant that as author he was everyone, including the heroine's cat, because he imagined and created all of them.

Ciao,
A

Lemme think. What I told her is probably the best way to put it. Sometimes, when you're creating and developing characters in a novel, it's like moving chess pieces around: it's hard to read what's going on inside of them behind that impassive sculpted wooden or ivory face, especially the horse who always poses as a lordly knight.

August 16, 2017

Dear Amadeo,

Well I have to admit that during the first week of my holidays I got very few messages from Sandro.

And I was upset about that and also about the quality of the message.

Sometimes he forgets that he can have me just with one sweet little word...

How many realities can I work with? The one within the epistolary email romanza, or the one outside of it.

Povera Sofia, poor Sofia, is emotionally enslaved to Sandro. He can do what he wants, she gets mad, like she has written, and then he wins her back with one sweet little word.

Enough is enough. I'm going to tell her she has to reassess her feelings, for they are being tossed around. Callously. Likely it's the sex that magnetizes her. Again, it might be geographic temperament: the sunny south vs. the chilly north.

Wait a minute. I've got the guys mixed up. It's her husband Aarvo who is from the chilly Finny north, not Sandro. But maybe I did this because I think of Sandro as a cold person, radiating chill.

On the second week of my holidays Sandro was back at the office and more free to communicate with me. Then we finally saw each other on Tuesday and today...

And today I had this nice feeling...

But you are so right and you have too good memory!!

I'm quite surprised about the fact that you didn't know the ending of your book when you first began to write. I thought all authors know the ending right away.

I'm so fascinated about the creation's process of a book, how it evolves from an idea to the result of a published novel!

So you could actually have created a different ending, maybe you will use it in the Russian or the Swedish edition, where perhaps Professor Shultish does get la ragazza yemenita.

That ending, that variation, I never thought of. And even had I thought of it, I wouldn't have used it. Never. That would have been too authorly manipulative. Absolutely *falsh*.

But your ending, dear Amadeo, at least in the Italian version, it's so much better.

Sometimes I daydream of something happening in my story with Sandro to shake things...but I can invent whatever ending to this, my, story, can't I???

Ciaoooo,
Sofia

How about me? Can I too, the alleged inventor [par excellence, the *nar* in me forces me to say], can I too invent an ending for her ro-manza according to *my* wishes? In this letter too she slides from roman to romanza.

Can't resist a bit of punning and self-immolation: I used "nar" as shortcut for narrator. But "nar" is also the Yiddish word for fool or jerk. Truth is, just the opposite. I meant "nar" as fool at the outset and only then did I notice it's the first sound of "narrator."

17 agosto 2017

Dear Sofia,

I have held off telling you this, but I'm not going to hold off any longer:

I am going to be absolutely frank, that is: honest, with you.

Direct.

You don't realize how often Sandro upsets you. Just reread your emails to me and you will see. You have to finally reassess your feelings toward him, for they are being tossed around, callously.

You can invent whatever ending you want to your romanza, but I urge you to remember the flippant answer Sandro once gave you, when you said, "Surely we will burn in hell," he said, "Yes." And also remember the constant mood of depression you are in, which lifts only on occasion, and then drops down low again.

And yet in a previous letter you said you "are more close...and more in love."

But I did not get this impression from the negative remarks you have been writing. What makes you say more in love? Suppose someone would say to you, prove it. Analyze it objectively.

You probably don't realize, but after reading so many romanzas you should know: women love love and are in love with love.

You also have to consider your heart health. Studies

have shown that emotional problems, stress in relationships, can cause narrowing of the arteries and produce
heart attacks. The heart has long been associated with
love and sadness and fear and courage (that word comes
from the Latin word "cor" for heart, like coronary). So be
careful. Or **corful**. Sometimes the heart tells you what you
feel and sends you warnings.

So I will close with the same thought that I began this
letter: with all the problems he has given you, you have to
step back and reassess your feelings.

Warmly,
Amadeo

◯ᗡᥱ

August 20, 2017

Caro,
You were in my thoughts these last days and probably
the universe sent them to you, and probably because I
received the thought you sent me.

I'm overwhelmed by the things I have to do at home
and with Neemi. I have the feeling I'm running and running. Jogging in place. Getting nowhere.

At home things are often difficult and I wonder what
should I do to fix this situation but while thinking I stay still.
Immobile. Like a car with the engine off.

Then there is Sandro. We had mini break together visiting a small town in a valley. We actually stayed at a b&b

which had photos all over from movie scenes that were shot at their place. The both owners were so proud.

That's a stunning, inadvertent pun: mini break. At first, seeing that phrase I thought they broke up for a brief period. But then I realized— that's what I wanted to see. But it was just the opposite. They took a break together.

About the relationship with Sandro, I alternate moments of total happiness to moments of emptiness and pain.

And she doesn't realize that this is the signature pattern of her love. Her love life. Happiness/pain. And re my last admonishing letter—no reaction.

I wish only that Sandro's wife runs away with a guy and gets out of my way. A nice turn in this story! What a laugh. The betrayed wife screwing the milkman!! Ha ha.

Anyway I have to get a grip of my life. Aarvo busy on his silkworm project, which is another source of stress for me. I must find out the way to get the best out of this life and not having the feeling that this life is running me instead.

Change the first "n" for "i" and you have a more apropos word for Sofia's life.

> But tell me also about you!! Are you on some new writ-
> ing's projects??
>
> Sofia.
> PS.

I wonder what I can say in reply. From a fictional or a realistic point of view, there isn't the slightest opening for me. Sofia is, according to her letter, in the middlest range of middling neutrality. She is in absolute stasis. Neither here nor there. So what can I do to tip the balance? When Sandro is indifferent, mean or flippant with her, I can criticize him and elevate myself. But with the present situation, the *mise-en-scene* is grey as fog, barely seen. But yet, it's still full of complications.

And this is the first time Sofia has mentioned Sandro's wife in a realistic fashion, aside from that photo of her that Sandro showed Sofia. Now there's one more character on stage in this real-life drama.

Sofia is continually hurting herself. Masochism. Never thought of that word before. Now it came to me. And it fits. Perfectly. And her phrase: getting nowhere. That's my word for her. Did the universe send that key word to her too?

Speaking of universe, happenings there affect me. A year ago, astronomers discovered space-time ripples created by colliding black holes. They heard black holes dancing in the dark, a jig choreographed by gravitational waves. This knocked astrophysicists upside down. It confirmed for the first time the existence of those waves and black holes, which until then had only theoretical support, with Einstein predicting this in his theory of relativity a hundred years earlier. When space and time are fluid, time bends. Can then past and future blend? If reality and unreality change places, that warm, marble-shaped flame Sofia had given me could be absolutely real.

Black holes squeeze lots of matter into a small space. The resulting gravitational pull is so intense anything that passes nearby, even light, is trapped forever.

Hopefully, not like Sofia with Sandro.

And more. There is a force called dark energy that is making the universe expand faster. A new study suggests that dark energy is getting stronger and denser, leading to a future wherein atoms are ripped apart and time ends. Again, hopefully, not before I meet Sofia again.

Then I read her PS.

Lately, before I go to sleep, I have been noticing something strange. It seems to me I have glasses on and yet when I bring my hand to my eyes to remove them, they are not there. I had already taken them off some time earlier. Can you explain this? You have such good insites.

Aug. 20, 2017

Dear Sofia,

No, I have no new project now. Your letters are my current writing project.*

And you? Have you stepped out of yourself and reassessed your frustrating situation, as I wrote to you recently?

I think you should.

You must.

With affection and concern,

A.

*Which is the truth, in an extended fashion. I'm thinking about her letters, her situation. Her. And me. Mulling.

Aug 27, 2017

Caro Amadeo,

The funny coincidence was that last night I was talking about you to an Irish scientist who wants to retire here in Parma.

I was telling him about your novel La Ragazza Yemenita and that he should read it. Later on I get your email. Telepathy??

Things have been really hectic around here. Doing housework and keeping track of silkworm orders. I can't get a grip on my life and I have the feeling that I'm rolling like a stone. Last few weeks have been very heavy for me.

In some languages "heavy" and "hard" is the same word. Sofia no doubt means the latter.

I did not write a bit of my memoir to you during the last week because I don't want you to see this darker version of me, you have this radiant image of Sofia and I tried to preserve it.

This may appear as an excuse but when I'm not feeling great I have the tendency to hide. Sorry about that.

I read, understand, what you say about stepping back. But it is so hard. I have stepped in so deep.

Love. There are moments when I feel so much in love, when I could do anything and I still dream of a life together. Other day I wish I had the "balls" (sorry for this) to send everybody to hell.

But apparently I don't have the guts. And I'm delaying. On all levels of my life.

But tell me also about you. What are you busy doing? When you go to NY what do you do, who do you see??

Don't you have some ideas for a new novel? I hope you still write.

And a curiosity: when is your birthday??

I promise that I will write more, somehow it's cathartic for me to write, I feel better after doing it. I hope you're not disappointed by the tone of my email.

I'm a natural complainer but I hope that my positive attitude comes out anyway.

Arrivederci,
Sofia

PS I wrote you last time about me sometimes feeling glasses on my nose and around my eyes but there is nothing there. But you did not answer.

Well, at least she is still showing some interest in me. And my birthday too. We have never mentioned birthdays before. Maybe she wants to send me something for my birthday. But to this I won't respond. It's nice that she's prodding me about writing. If she only knew what an idea for a novel I'm thinking about, slowly, developing.

And her wish to have the guts, balls, to send everyone to hell, that's good news. She's trying, whether she knows it or not, to loosen herself from the bonds of...

Of what?

But she's stuck into her affair. Stepped in deep, as she says. Another vulgar Americanism comes to mind. And it fits her situation perfectly. How can I get her to extricate herself?

That glasses phenomenon is puzzling. I'll give it some thought.

Aug 27, 2017

Cara Sofia,

I don't see you as a complainer. You are just a faithful reporter, chronicling reality. Boy, you have never asked so many questions. I rarely go to NY.

I hope you are well.

Do keep writing. And I appreciate so much your interest in, and concern for, my writing. Indeed, I've been thinking about something, but I don't like to talk about a project until it's finished.

Best,
Amadeo

PS The truth is, cara cara Sofia, that from your dark letters I can't help but see the dark side of you. This whole affair is making you dark. But since I only have a mental photo of the one time I saw you in the bright Italian June sunshine—smiling, beaming, full of humor, exuding life and allure and, yes, sexiness—that's the image I always have of you in my mind, and not the darker one that comes forth from this hapless love affair you have stumbled into. Stepped into so deep.

Sorry about the delay in writing about that fascinating experience of yours with imagined glasses. You remember Socrates's famous dictum: the unexamined life isn't worth living? That's what's happening to you. I'm no psychologist, but I think you're imagining glasses to look into, to examine yourself. And those "glasses" you occasionally sense, it's as if you're saying to yourself: I have to look into myself and my situation more carefully. Scrutinize myself. And you must do this; otherwise, the rest of Socrates's ominous words start to pertain.

August 29, 2017

Caro Giorgio,

I read and reread your letters. You are so smart. I also appreciate that you are not afraid of being frank with me. While it hurts a bit to read your direct words, I know they have to be said. Because on my own I would not think of them. The curtain is pulled too tight over my eyes. And thanks for that wonderful "glasses" analysis.

Lately I have had to some traveling, doing that silk-worm business work for Aarvo, and when I'm free I try to enjoy my little boy.

I think often of you* and I long for some time for myself but clearly it's not now.

Tomorrow I'm off to Naples and next week I will be in Paris. I will find a moment to write again. I need to put my thoughts black on white and let them create my life.

I really believe in the creative power of words. When you write it's a statement you send to the world. Aren't words wonderful? Anyway I'm getting off the subject...

Baci Baci
Sofia

PS I long for always-ness, not once-in-a-while-ness. Maybe I should tell this to Sandro. But maybe not, because I know what his answer will be.

*Those words make me feel so good. I weigh the emotional heft of "I think often of you," and Sandro is mentioned only in the PS, and so the intimacy of her words is enhanced, and another warm link is created, something like a clasp of hands. And when I think of the words "warm link," at once, of its own accord, the warm little flame shaped like a little marvel, oh my God, what a great typo for marble, that Sofia gave me from her heart first time we met comes back to me. I feel it in the palm of my right hand, but I dare not look at it. It radiates a lovely warmth that spreads throughout my body like loving words. And these words stand high and glow over the dull phrases citing where Sofia will be traveling.

Her letter is more to my liking. She's back to calling me Giorgio. And closes with a double set of kisses.

Aug 29, 2017

Cara Sofia,

You remarked, aren't words wonderful? They sure are. Even the spaces between them, and punctuation too is a marvel. I recently wrote the following lines about words and language, and I'll share it with you. I'm sure you'll like this.

I wrote in my sketchbook:

We think words make up language. Not so. Words are the wheels; punctuation, the engine. Take the well-known combination of "don't" and "stop." It is the punctuation and silence that signals the difference between prudery and lascivity.

Look at the difference between these two sentences.

A woman, speaking to a guy, says: "I don't want you to! Stop!"

She doesn't like what he's doing and she's telling him to stop.

Now take this same sentence, with the very same words, but with a slightly different punctuation.

"I don't want you to stop."

She loves what he's doing and tells him to continue, not to even think of stopping.

Another version could be: "Don't! Leave me alone!"

With its opposite: "Don't leave me alone."

If you look at it closely, objectively, language is exaggeration. Every time a line is said or written, it's exaggeration. It's an enigma: writing both condenses and exaggerates life.

All best, baci,
Giorgio

And I think to myself, I can hear her saying, Don't leave me alone, which prompts the thought: I've got to see her. Should I fly to Parma and surprise her? But first I have to make sure she's there. And not in Naples or Paris. Oh, if I only knew Sandro's place of work or phone number.

Would Sofia join me if I invited her to go away with me for a few days in Italy? She could tell both Sandro and Aarvo that she's on some kind of research trip.

August 31, 2017

Caro caro Amadeo,
Lately, for some reason, I speak a lot about you and your book.

I'm a sort of one man PR of your work.

I know that my writting to you is drasticly short, but to write nicely takes time and I'm running out of this precious item. Time.

I've been involved more and more with silkworms and I'm trying to slow down, to try to have some time with my son, to organize social get together with friends, call my father and mother every day, and at night I drop on a couch exhausted. I have a pile of books to read by my bed, dust on them.

I'm not saying it out loud but I don't like my life how it is, how it became, but I don't know how to change it. I stay still in this craziness, and I feel like a Guinea pig in a cage. Awful image.

You know I want to be a photographer, take pictures of small details in the streets, of faces.

Buy a damn camera Sofia and go around and make photos.

I feel trapped by all the silkworm responsibilities, the knowledge that the love of my life will never leave his wife, that my husband will never be the right person for me, that life goes by too fast.* But my dea Amadeor,** do you want really to read this?

I wish I could share splendid stories with *** and not this outpouring of a neurosis.

I will try to find some space and time for me, and share some moments with you.

Thanks for your patience and for reading me!

Un abbraccio,
Sofia

* I feel so bad reading this. But what can I do except commiserate? There are no magic strings I can pull to slow down her life, to free her of Aarvo, to make Sandro leave his wife. Or is there another magic string called wings? Reading her words makes me want to hop on a plane and fly to her and tell her I want to talk talk talk to her, spend some time with her. In her current low state, she might agree. The line

between Platonism and romanza is not made of wire. And given her constant complaints about her love life and her "always thinking of you," who knows? The verbal abbraccio may turn into a physical one. With feeling.

New stuff here in this letter. Surprises. Socializing. Never heard that word before.

Another thing: till now Sofia had never mentioned parents. So busy with boyfriend, never spoke of mama or papa. Also a first: photography. She summed up her lover/husband problem with one long sentence, with "trapped" and two "never"s, one for Sandro, one for Aarvo.

** In her first draft, Sofia called me just "my dear." Then she must have rethought that chilly endearment and inserted "Amadeo"—but she put it in too hastily, inserted it right toward the end of "dear" and that's why the "dear" was split up and it came out as: "dea Amadeor."

*** In her typing excitement, she left out the word "you" after "share splendid stories with."

Sept 1, 2017

Dear, dear Amadeo,

Now with my experience as a silkworm "expert," I've gotten a new job with the International Silk Worm Association. It was a job Aarvo was suppose to have but since he hardly works now, so busy with his silkworm book I got it.

I work absurd hours, but we need the money now, and when I get home from that little office they have given me, I'm so tired I'm just the shadow of myself. Some health problems are annoying me lately and all this seems just like a bad story! But you'll be glad to hear I've gone back to the gym after being away for a long time. It really feels good to exercise. I do it every day from 11 am to noon.

I really would love to write more longly and tell nice episodes of my life or thoughts, but they are lost in the caos of this life of mine.

Aarvo is very happy with what he is accomplishing with his book.

Sometimes I wish that Aarvo, like me, has a romanza on the side, and is pondering when to leave me. But, my luck, he too, like Sandro, doesn't want to break up the family. So even if Aarvo is having a love affair, which I doubt, it isn't doing me any good. All I can hope for is for Sandro's wife to be having some kind of affair.

And I sort of tongue-in-cheek think of telling Sofia, "If she's as charming, good-looking and sexy as you, I'll oblige." But what would that accomplish for me? Nothing. Except firm up the relationship between Sofia and Sandro.

The other half of my life, the one that is hidden, is pretty much the same as when we met. I have asked Sandro if, one day, maybe, there would be a chance for us, but apparently he doesn't have the courage to leave his family.

Sometimes I understand, sometimes not, and sometimes I just refuse to understand. Till the day I have the corage to put the word "end" to this fairy tale.

I'm at the airport now, in Bologna, I go for couple of days in Finland to pick up my son who had been spending a week with his grandpa in Helsinki, then I will return and go back to Sicily, like last year, with family for two weeks.

There is much more to say and to tell, but they are starting with boarding soon.

It makes me feel special that you still inquire for me and I will try my best to write more often. I hope you love your life! I will too, very soon.

Abbracci,
Sofia

PS Can't help it. I keep thinking of my love. Tell me, can define love?

Did she purposely spell "corage" without the "u" to reflect what I wrote to her re the link between courage and heart/coronary? Or is it simply a mistake?

And what word follows "can"? We? You? I write her a quick note and say:

Cara, love is a two-way street, or better, a lovely, aromatic, tree-lined path that two negotiate, preferably with birds tweeting, and an occasional hummingbird that the two enjoy together. Otherwise, it's a dark alley that you stumble on alone. All alone.

To which Sofia thanked me, writing:

What a brilliant insight. Only a poet like you—who creates characters and knows so much about the human heart—could express such beautiful thoughts.

And I write back to her:

Cara Sofia,
By reminiscing about your love, it seems you want to possess, hold on to, your past.

A.

Sept 1, 2017

Cara Sofia,
I hope you are well and thinking good thoughts, positive thoughts, hopeful thoughts, to counteract those thoughts that make you feel down. It's good, great, to hear you're exercising. Good for body, good for spirit.
With all good wishes, and thanks for your nice words on my definition of love.
Any plans for visiting the USA?

Amadeo

PS For the first time in your letter—I reread last ones

carefully—I saw the word "end." And when I saw that word I jumped up and shouted, "Hooray!" Brava! Finally. It takes **cor**age to think and print that word. It hurts me to give you sad advice. But you will have to say, loud and clear: **END.** If Sandro won't break up his family, isn't that a definitive signal for you?

Here's an idea. For both Aarvo and Sandro's wife to have an affair, why don't you introduce, or get Sandro somehow to introduce, his wife to your husband. Or get Sandro's wife to introduce me to you.

It seems to me that life has gone out of her letters. Even in complaint there had been an endearing vibrancy to them. But of late, they sound as if the life has been sucked out of the words, the letters, and the spaces between the letters. Excitement a foreign word. And my hope re her positive thoughts is thoroughly banal too.

Dear Sofia,

A quick PS note. You know, you never told me your husband's last name.

I.e., how do they call you? Mrs. _____?

And just out of curiosity (you said you love my curiosity), what is Sandro's family name? You said he lives in a small town near Parma? Which one?

Thanks and all best,

A.

∽

And Sofia answered immediately:

Sept 1, 2017

Caro Amadeo,

Sure. Family name is Sibelius. No, no. No relation whatsoever to the great composer.

And Sandro's last name is Martinello. He lives near Parma in a small town, Tabiano. Since he works as an independent insurance adjustor, that gives him flexible time (to sometimes spend with me).

You're so funny. Your comedic introductions made me laugh out loud. What a imagination.

Sofia

PS Would love to visit USA but now impossible.

I just knew it about Sandro. Predicted early on he'd be the insurance type.

∽

Sept 2, 2017

Dear Amadeo,

Thank you for being there and listening to my struggles!

I know that all starts with me and I have very little influence on circumstances.

I have to work harder on myself.

As per me, I have good days altering with other where I wonder why I let my reptilian brain take over. I always considered myself as a woman who used her brain, just did not realize that I'm using the wrong part of it.

I should have all my thought processed by my neurocortex, but unfortunately amygdala takes over. I'm a overcharged loaded bomb of emotions. I feel anger, jealousy, resentment, love, hate...

Maybe I'm just—remember? I once wrote a sentence this way—human.

    Sofia

She sure surprised me with these fancy anatomical words. Wow. Amygdala. First time she drives me to the dictionary. Where did she learn sophisticated terms like that? Another first: her using the word "hate."

Sept 5, 2017

Dear A,
Listen to this:
Yesterday I was at the train station waiting on the plat-
form to leave for Naples
I was eating an ice cream and then I felt that someone
was looking at me. I turned and it was Sandro. He passed
by just to kiss me goodbye. It was a very nice moment.
Very brief but very intense.

Baci,
Sofia

Sept. 5, 2017

Caro,
Writing again.
Tomorrow I will leave for Sicily to join Neemi and Aarvo.
Two weeks off trying to recover from the fatigue of
these months. But before leaving I wanted to share this
sort of "movie" I play, sometimes, in my head and also
shared with Sandro. To scare the hell out of him.
Sandro's dad has a vegetable garden some km away
from his home. He loves to go there and grow vegetables.
He has some chickens and a little hut with a veranda.
I have been there couple of times with Sandro. It's a
very bucolic place.

Last night Sandro told me that they were having dinner at the "orto" with all the family (his and hers too), a
summer get together.

So now please follow my imagination, my "movie"...
See this "orto" with some cats wandering around, a simple
table, not maching chairs, a bench and a veranda. Some
wine, cheese on the table. Kids running after the cats.

A car drives by. It stops. People are talking but some
stop because they heard the car. It's me who gets out of
the car and enters the "orto" by this small gate (where
normally there is a lock). I walk a few steps to arrive at the
veranda.

At this moment they are all silent. A deathly quiet. As if
all sounds turned off.

They don't know what going on. And they don't know
me.

So I look at Sandro and say, "Do you introduce me or
shall I do it??"

Further silence.

I'm Sofia, I say. In this absolute silence my words do
not have to be loud.

Wish I could write nice stories as you do...But this is
the "movie" I imagine.

Baci,
Sofia

And I respond with a short note: "Sofia, this is imaginative, post-
mod fiction. A great magic realism scene. I can just picture it."

Yet all I feel is pity.

Sept 6, 2017

Dear Sofia,
I hope you are well and feeling good in Sicily.
Now here is some news.
I hope to be in Parma again, very likely end September, and I hope you will be hope and not traveling, and we will be able to see each other and spend some time together.

With all good wishes,
A

Oh, my Lord! I wrote *hope* instead of *home.* again psyche-driven typos. Shows how much hope I have in her direction.

Sept. 6, 2017

Caro Amadeo,
How wonderful news from you! Yes, I'll be home. Just confirm dates.
On my side, not much to tell, apart from too much worries.
But I'm trying very hard not to let circumstances affect my good humor and my joie de vivre. Sometimes it's very

hard but I'm a fighter.

Saluti carissimi,
Look forward to see you soon,
Sofia

That "carissimi" sent a glow of warmth through me. She didn't write the more distant "caro," "dear," but the affectionate "carissimi"—"my little dear one," a warm, intimate, loving word that I can hold in the palm of one hand while I hold her little flame in the palm of the other. Coupled with that "look forward to see you soon," imagine what that did to the lifeblood flowing through my veins.

September 6, 2017

Dear Sofia,
Here's the latest re my travel plans to see you.
I'll be in Parma for three days the last days of the month.

Best wishes,
A.

Less and less to comment on. I hope Sofia is truly as excited to see me as I am to see her.

September 7, 2017

Caro Amadeo,
My life has been a real roller coaster lately.
Aarvo has again gone on a silkworm eggs trip to Japan. He will be gone for a while, and I have been handling more of his work, Neemi, and household on my own.
Things with Sandro are on hold. We still have contact but since he told me recently that he would never leaves his wife, I don't think there is much to add. I still love him dearly but I'm very disappointed.
I'll be here in Parma at the end of the month and all October and I hope we can see each other and chat.*
Please let me know if you'll have time for lunch together.

Sofia

*Sofia's letter (back to "Caro" again) brought me down from the high of her "carissimi" salutation of the other day. And more, her chill tone (I actually felt grainy snowflakes on my skin) extinguished that revived little flame she had given me. Worse, her cold and abrupt "chat" gave me a little *tsvick* in my heart. All the words before "chat"—"I hope we see each other"—seemed to be heading to an invitation I had in mind, like "spend some time together," but that wished-for phrase did not appear. And "lunch" jabbed at me too. Just lunch? Just talking? Three thousand miles (one way) just for a meal?

But on the bright side, re: her love affair with Sandro, it looks like it's over.

⌒ℬℯ

Sept. 7, 2017

Dear Sofia,
Still would like to hear from you as to whether we can spend some time together when I am in Parma on Sept 28, 29, 30. I'd like to see you more than just for lunch. Lunch is just so short. I'm coming in for only one reason
To see you.
Period.
Punto, as you once said in a letter.

Should I say it? I mused. Yes. I will.

I'm not traveling 6000 miles round trip for lunch. We've spent so many hours together writing to each other, reading each other, it would be astonishing if when we have a chance to see each other in person, it's just for lunch.
Be well, and hope to see you soon.

A.

⌒ℬℯ

September 7, 2018

Caro Amadeo,

I would love to see you in Parma. Last Monday and Tuesday of the month would would be perfect for me. I will take off from work and I'll take you to a restaurant whose new young and very talented chef comes from my village close to Modena.

If this plan work for you we could meet at around 12:30 on Monday. Looking forward to seeing you and spending time with you. But first better we talk by phone—right?—to make the plans good. So sorry about the shortness atmosphere of chat.

Baci baci ed abbracci
Sofia

Two days off. That's better news. Maybe "chat" in her previous email was a cover word, a sort of self-protection. Still, is that the only thing she can think of—eating? Why focus on food? Still, her "sorry" is welcome. And even more, that line: "Looking forward to seeing you and spending time with you." That I like.

A lot.

And the double kiss and embrace just before her name.

Sept 9, 2017

Dear Sofia,

Wonderful to hear from you. That's good news, perfect news, about your two days free.

I will arrive late on Saturday (a day earlier than I had planned because of ticket problems) and stay at Hotel Parma Uno. And I will call you next morning. But hopefully we can speak before then.

So our first meeting could take place on Monday, as per your note.

But you know what? Best thing is to finalize everything over the phone. I'll call you a few days before I arrive.

Hope to see you soon. I too am looking forward to seeing you.

A.

I will very likely arrive a few days prior to that date to try out some ideas burbling in my head, but I'm not going to share that with Sofia.

Sept 9, 2017

Cara Sofia,
PS to my previous letter.
Just want to tell you, when I see you, like the day we

met at the Parma beach and then said goodbye, I'm going to kiss you on your **house of worship**.

A.

Sept 9, 2017

Caro Amadeo,
What's this? I don't remember that, and I don't know *house of worship*. What kind of body part is that? Is that American slang for something?

Baci,
Sofia

Sept 9, 2017

Cara Sofia,
No, it ain't American slang for anything.
Do you know a synonym for house of worship?

A.

Caro A,
Well, I know of church? But do I have a church you can kiss? I might have a cross, but I know you're not going to kiss that.

S.

What's interesting in this exchange of emails all during the same day is that Sofia is not once protesting or complaining about or distancing herself from that delectable verb.

In fact, by articulating, "do I have a church you can kiss," she is perhaps even stating that if she *had* a church I could kiss it, no problem.

Cara Sofia,
You're getting too religiously sectarian. No, you don't have a church, but you do have a dictionary.
Look up synonym for a non-sectarian place to pray.
And if you don't have a dictionary try the internet.

Amadeo

Caro Amadeo,
This is fun. I don't have a mosque nor a synagogue either.

S.

And I imagine her still wondering: Where in heaven's name on a woman's body is that house of worship?

Cara Sofia,
Here's another hint. If one gets a mild dose of religion (and/or a good synonym finder), it's a place where one can find a place to express one's non-sectarian devotion.
There is still one more word which means house of worship but you haven't gotten it yet.
The same place I kissed you when I said goodbye to you and gave you that nice goodbye hug.

Amadeo

Dear Amadeo,
I give up. Please tell me. My dictionary has given up too. That makes two of us.

I'm holding up two hands in surrender, but that dictionary is dam heavy.

Also, I don't fully understand your long sentence with "express" and "non-sectarian devotion" but you write so beautifully.

Sofia

Cara Sofia,
Okay. I guess if you surrender I'll have to give you the answer. The "house of worship" where I kissed you is the temple. Just in front of the ear.
Now do you remember?

A.

Caro Amadeo,
Now I get it. You word worshiping raskel.

Grazie mille,
Sofia

And, yes, I do remember.

Now for the question, how to get to her. To socialize. Beyond "chats." Once she sees me I feel her attitude will change. Is changing. For those "house of worship" exchanges were quite positive. Even flirtatious. Her affection for me was, is, already locked into all her letters. It began with that first hug I gave her when we parted a few months ago at the Parma beach, with me putting my arms around her, holding her close, and kissing her temple just near her left eye. And Sofia couldn't possibly erase all those words she had written to me in all her letters, baci, kisses without end, and abbracci, hugs galore, unless they were all false. They were all addressed to me. Whether it was to me as her listener, her confessor, or me as the creator of those characters in a book she liked so much. (And altar ego would go well with a temple.)

By now two points were in my favor.

1) Sofia's husband, Aarvo, had already discovered her duplicity by reading her emails to Sandro.

2) Sofia continually complained about Sandro's duplicity, even though she never used that word.

But so pissed off was Sofia at Sandro for his hesitation, for his assertion that he'd never leave his wife, that she even castigated herself for not telling him, in her words, "to fuck off." Where she learned that thoroughly American Anglo-Saxonism still floors me, unless she spent some time in the USA that she had never told me about. I suppose it could also have come from films or books.

Of course, all the above might go out the window if all along Sofia has been considering me a sort of older brother. But I'm negating that with everything I have sensed till now, especially that avian mating dance Sofia did before me, or better: *for* me, on the Parma beach first day we met, when she took off her light blue terrycloth robe and showed me her sumptuous body clad only in an orange bikini. And that warm flame compressed into a little marble that—it still, still seems to me—she plucked from her heart and presented to me.

I could wait for her to act when I got to Parma, which might take a long time, for I see how slow her reactions are to the problems Sandro has been giving her. Or I could take the initiative. Then I recall Aarvo's in Japan for a while, so there's a good chance he won't be home when I'm in Parma. There's a third point in my favor.

Sofia's almost slavish attachment to Sandro makes me wonder if he could have cast such a magic spell over her, or, to paraphrase Cresside's memorable words in Chaucer's *Troilus and Cresside*, "Who hath given me drinke?" Or was boyfriend Sandro such a great stud and husby Aarvo such a Finnish dud that Sofia's pleasure canceled all the other long and looming negatives?

Was it possible for me to somehow become Sandro? Reading Sofia's letters about him made me fuse with him and, for a while, I thought I was him. And by becoming Sandro I felt an enchanted silk scarf over me and sensed my affection for Sofia even more intensely. So in this aerie level, I had to combine my looking at her through a double set of eyes: mine and the ones I had arrogated from Sandro.

Sofia did say, "Wonderful to hear your voice." She did say, "You are a darling, Amadeo, can't tell you that enough." She did say, just the other day, "Looking forward to spending some time with you." Are those platonic words? Or can that thin platonic film be easily stripped away?

I already had her affection; if not of the heart, then surely of the spirit and mind. And the path between heart and spirit/mind was not a thorny one. For some, the flesh sufficed. For the (s)elect few, the mind led the charge and eased open closed doors. What's more, she looked up to me. That's a given. She loved books, reading, literature, and I was not only an author, but the author of a book she had read and adored and constantly asked questions about. The author who, to her surprise and delight, was sitting there right next to her on the Parma beach.

But awe is one thing. Affection another. Still, with her epistolary sign-off kisses, hugs, thinking often of me, even that warm "Yours," and that memorable "carissimi," Sofia quite likely loved me in a certain way, on a certain level. And then—I can't help bringing it up, reminding myself of it, puzzling if it was real or only a dream, but her hand going to her heart and giving me that magical warm flame. That, I'll never forget.

I wonder if there was a love intent, perhaps even subconscious, when Sofia gave me that little flame. Did she mean by that what I thought she meant? Sofia is Italian, and in her language "little flame" was *fiammetta*, a word she would surely know. And second, her close link to Boccaccio's *Decameron* just glided into my head, the book that Sandro had given her years ago, when they first met. A book Sofia treasured, the very *Decameron* wherein Boccaccio's own love is referred to as Fiammetta.

So if one—that is, me, I, your editor/translator—weaves these various strands together, one—okay, *I*—cannot help but to conclude, an awkward, circumlocuitous way of saying, "I'm quite sure," that that little flame Sofia once plucked from her heart and gave me was a pointed, multilayered, multidimensional reference to her amore for me.

By handing me that little flame, that *fiammetta*, Sofia was declaring that just as Boccaccio loved his little Fiammetta, Sofia was, is, presenting that little love flame, that *fiammetta*, to me.

With this in mind, I brush aside, broom-swoosh away, the thought that wishful thinking can vivify the unreal. And never mind the swift chill built into that little flame. For how long can one hold a marble-sized flame in one's palm, even if it's a beloved little *fiammetta*, before being burned?

But this I did know: the time for me to act would be in Parma. In person. Because despite Sofia's incessant complaints about Sandro's hesitancy, she did nothing about it. Despite my constant suggestions.

So if she wouldn't, didn't, act—*I* would.

And not via emails.

In an arena where duplicity was a legitimate tool—even a weapon—I'd have to make use of it too. Sofia was using duplicity. Sandro was using duplicity. I'd be the third, and since I'd be involved with three players, I would do triplicity and hope that all these (il)licities would not trip me up.

But how to go about it?

I sat in a chair, closed my eyes, made believe I was already in Parma, and began to think. Suppose this was a romanza and I was a character in it, what devices would I use to achieve my goal? Or if I were the writer, how would I manage the plot in this character's favor?

Also, how could I slyly interact with the three other characters in this romanza—Sofia, Sandro, and Aarvo, four with Sandro's wife—and still keep my anonymity?

Maybe I better consult with the Professor Ezra Shultish and ask him what plans he had to get the Yemenite girl.

Sitting still with closed eyes is a good move. And making believe it's an unfolding story I'm writing was even better.

Soon, little by little, a whole bunch of scenarios, in fact seven of them, played out in my mind's eye. And then, so as not to lose them, I jotted them down as if they were part of a rough draft of a manuscript.

ONE:

I COULD CALL AARVO the Finn. Sofia said Aarvo is in Japan, probably doing his silkworm eggs, and would be gone for "a while." But for how long? Let's assume he's back home when I'm in Parma and I speak to him and pretend I'm Sandro.

No, that won't work. Even if my Italian were good, he'd recognize a non-Italian accent. I could say I was an Englishman and that an Italian friend of mine—yes, that might work—asked me to apologize to you, to confess that he did wrong in having an affair with your wife, Sofia.

I would have to say I'm an English friend because if I said American, he might suspect it was me, the writer in the USA with whom Sofia was sharing some stories.

On second thought that won't work either, because after husband Aarvo confronted wife Sofia, she'd call Sandro and he would deny the truth of that incident, for what friend of his would possibly pull a trick like that? And Sandro would say he doesn't even have any Englishman friends. That scenario might worsen the Aarvo-Sofia relationship and could even drive Sofia closer to Sandro.

On third thought I'd have to have Aarvo's cell number which I don't have. And calling a landline is no good because Sofia might answer.

And, finally, why should I hurt Sofia with such a stupid phone call.

TWO:

HERE'S A BETTER ONE. Since Sofia's husband, the Finn, spoke with an accent anyway, I could call Sandro, pretend I'm Aarvo, and tell Sandro I'm talking in English because Italian is not my native language and that I can better express myself in English: I know all about the affair you're having with my wife, and you better disappear, or else, etc. Yes, that's a much better choice.

When Sofia reports this dramatic turn of events to me, she says Sandro told her that Aarvo called and threatened him and Sandro's afraid even to email her anymore. And Sofia wonders how Aarvo was able to get to Sandro. She suspects Sandro is making this up. "Maybe it's better this way," Sofia says. "I didn't have the balls" (yes, that's the word she had used) "to make the break myself, so it's perfectly sensible that he did."

And I'd say, "I'm flying over even sooner than I planned."

"You are?" she says with a hoped-for bit of joy in her voice.

"Yes. At once. Soon as I can get a ticket. You need to talk. You need a shoulder."

And I'll give you other body parts as well, I didn't say.

"You are a perfect darling. Send details and I'll pick you up at the airport."

"No need for that," I said, since I was already in Parma. "My publisher already paid for a taxi. I can't wait to see you." And I'd say it two or three times. Maybe just two.

But Sofia wonders, as do I, how come Aarvo is silent re: all this. Not a word out of him.

And, furthermore, how do I get to Sandro? I don't have his number. And how do I know he speaks English?

Plan #2, which sounded so delightful, is no good either.

THREE:

ANOTHER OPTION WOULD BE for me (pretending to be the Finn Aarvo) to call Sandro's home—he likely has a landline phone—and ask to speak to Sandro's wife. To her I say in my limited Italian, explaining that Finnish is my native language, that I have just discovered this affair between my wife, Sofia, and your husband. The wife would then lash out at Sandro for this, and he would contact Sofia and tell her that his wife has found out about them and she said that if this continues for one more day she would do something drastic. Sofia then tells me she got an email from Sandro that he regretfully has to stop seeing her.

A possibility. But I'd have to get Sandro's wife on the phone and also expand my limited Italian.

FOUR:

I CALL SOPHIA (WHO am I thinking of, spelling her name with "ph" instead of "f"?), change my voice to a higher pitch, pretend I'm Sandro's
wife, and tell her I know all about your affair with my husband, and
that if it doesn't stop I would kill either him or myself or both of us,
then you can raise the twins. And hang up.

Wait a minute. I can't speak Italian that well. And, anyway, if Sofia
recognized my voice that would ruin everything. Too chancy.

FIVE:

ANOTHER BRILLIANT IDEA. SINCE by now Aarvo already knows boy-friend Sandro's name, I call around 11:15 am, when I know Sofia is in the gym, and ask to speak to Mrs. Sibelius. Aarvo tells me she's not at home (just as I expected). He would ask me who is calling and what kind of message I wanted to leave. I would say, "Well, I'm not autho-rized to speak to anyone else, but since I obviously have someone from the household on the line, please tell Mrs. Sibelius that her reservation for her and Sandro Martinello at the hotel in Naples is confirmed."

That would make Aarvo angry, but it might not necessarily prompt a separation of Sandro and Sofia.

For that I'd have to sound Napolitan and here, again, have a richer vocabulary.

And, again, I'm being mean to Sofia.

SIX:

I CALL SANDRO'S WIFE, Mrs. Martinelli, pretend I'm Sofia, tell her I'm having an affair with her husband. He's been stringing me along for years and I can't take it anymore. Tell Sandro to make up his mind by next week. Either me or you. Not both of us.

Wait a minute...For this one too I would not only have to change my voice but also my accent, and here too I would need a wider-ranging Italian.

SEVEN:

I COULD CALL UP Sophia (oh my goodness, again Sophia), pretend I'm me, and tell her I'm crazy about her.

These were my seven options.
Whether I would act on even the least chancy of them is an open question.

I ARRIVED IN PARMA a few days before the date I had given Sofia and checked into the Hotel Parma Uno as planned. I called her, of course without revealing I was already in town, and made plans to meet.

In the hallway the next morning I met a chambermaid named Gina who spoke English. She was a pretty girl in her mid-twenties, with big brown eyes that had unusual tiny yellow flecks. Her demeanor and way of speaking indicated that this was a temporary job. Gina seemed to be way above the typical working class maid. And I noticed that she prettied up her impersonal uniform, a black dress with buttons down the middle tied with a narrow white belt and a white rounded collar, with a fine gold (or mock gold) necklace.

Remember, when I first saw Sofia's lovely face at the Parma beach months ago, I immediately thought of Sophia with a "ph"? Now too hearing the name Gina, I thought of another famous Italian Gina. Not that this Gina looked anything like the other one, but I love affinity, and the affinity of names always delights me.

As soon as I found out that Gina understood and spoke English, at once an idea came to me that put all my six or seven options, most of them quickly rejected, to shame. If I could evoke Gina's interest and get her cooperation, I had a hunch this new plan would succeed.

I introduced myself (I hoped for a moment that she, like Sofia, would recognize my name, but it did not happen), told her I was from the USA, then asked her:

"How is your English?"

"Not bad," Gina said. "To work here you have to know a bit of English. But I have studied too. Is there something you need?"

"Well, thank you for asking. Would you like to make some extra money?"

Soon as I said that, I regretted my words. She might misinterpret my intent.

I looked at Gina's face. Relieved that I didn't see any untoward reaction, I said quickly, "I need someone who understands English and speaks Italian, and I will compensate that person for a bit of work, which shouldn't take long."

"I can do that. What can I do to help you?"

"Well, I can't discuss it with you while you're working. It will take too long and I don't want to disturb you now. Do you get a break for lunch?"

"I start very early, at six thirty in the morning, and finish work at two thirty in the afternoon. I take only a fifteen-minute stop to have a sandwich and a cafe. But after two thirty I am free."

"Sounds good. Would you like...may I invite you to join me for a drink and pastries at that nice little pastry shop a few doors down, close to the corner?"

"Certainly," Gina said at once, nodding a couple of times. "Thank you. I know exactly the one you refer. But it will be a few minutes after two thirty, for I have to change from my work clothes."

"That will be fine. Thanks. I'll wait for you there. Inside the pastry shop."

Gina arrived at two forty. She looked around for a while, a serious mien on her face. Then, when she saw me, she waved and smiled. I confess, after two thirty-three, I looked both at my watch and at the door several times, wondering if she would show up.

Now she looked different. She wore dark green slacks and a char-treuse, short-sleeved sweater in the mild, end-September weather. Not that she didn't look good before, but out of uniform Gina looked even more eye-catching. She glowed. That little golden chain was still around her neck.

I couldn't help complimenting her. "What a cool outfit you're wearing, Gina."

"Well, it's actually warm still in Parma."

Then I realized she wasn't familiar with that slang term.

"The word 'cool' has a rather new American meaning, like great, terrific. Not chilly or cold. I meant to say it's a fine, becoming outfit."

"Well, it's more comfortable and, anyway, I can't wait to get out of that black, gloomy, impersonal maid's uniform and into normal clothes."

My compliment, I noticed, didn't elicit that typical American, "Thank you."

I showed her the menu and asked what she would like.

"Mmm. Everything looks so good."

"So take it all. Get whatever you like."

She chose a fruit platter and a cake, while I, so excited about talking to her and seeing if could interest her to play a role in my plan, could only sip a cup of tea.

While she was eating, I asked her, "This isn't your real job, is it?"

"Well, now it is a real job, but no, this is not my career. I am saving money to go to dental school."

"I'm so glad to hear that. Your smile will be a good advertisement for your work. Now as to why I need your help. I need your knowledge of English and Italian regarding a love problem—not mine. It's a prob-lem a woman friend of mine has."

"Oh!" Gina put down her fork and leaned forward.

I summed up for her the Sofia-Sandro relationship. I also told Gina that Sofia had written to me that she wished she could somehow write an END to this story. For Sandro had told her he would never leave his wife. And that's why I flew in to see if I could help. By the time I finished Gina knew the entire romanza.

"So nice of you to fly here to help her. Does Sofia know you're here?"

"Great question, Gina. You're a very astute girl."

"Astute. That you explain to me, please."

"Sure. Astute means wise, smart. Yes, she knows I am coming— but I came a few days early to work out some plans. So she doesn't know I am here now."

"And what am I supposed to do?"

"You're an important part of the plan. If you agree to play a role in my movie," and here I smiled, "without a camera, of course. Not only important, but you could very well be the crucial, the key player in this scenario, the star of the film. Indeed, the determining factor. If what you do works out, you may succeed where I have been unsuccessful..."

Then I outlined for Gina what role she would play, acting out my Plan #4.

I told her who she would pretend to be, whom she would be talking to, and what to say. I took out a notepad and wrote down the important lines she would say—"keep accenting the twins"—and what to expect to hear on the other side of the phone conversation.

"Oh, this is so exciting," Gina said.

"Looks like you're agreeing."

"Of course. What a movie this is!"

"Even without knowing who these people are, you would be doing a good deed and cause a little less anguish..."

"Anguish, don't know that..."

"Same word as deep worry, suffering."

"Ah."

"Less suffering for that person."

From her pocketbook, Gina took out a pen and notepad and made some jottings.

Then she took a deep breath and exhaled, as if shaking off stage fright before coming out to perform.

"Ready?"

"Yes."

And it was a firm, assured assent.

"Do you know her name?" Gina asked me. "What if Sofia asks me, What's your name?"

"Another great question. Boy am I glad I met you. If Sofia asks that question, you can say it's not important. You can say, 'If my husband never mentioned my name all these years, it's not important now...' And if another problem comes up, just cover the phone, and consult me. Ready now?"

"Yes," Gina said. "Can you understand my Italian?"

"I understand it better than speak it, but since I know the subject of the conversation, I'll be able to follow. And don't forget to say that you're using a borrowed phone because you don't want to be called back."

Gina nodded and said, "You know what? Let's make a rehearse."

"Okay, but let's talk a little softer. People at the other tables don't have to listen to our business."

And Gina automatically said at once, "Shh..." as if giving herself orders. "You know what, let's go outside to the little park in front of the hotel."

"Good idea." I paid the waiter and we went outside.

We sat down on a bench and pretended to be the players. The rehearsal went well. I even managed to go through the routine in my limited Italian.

"Ready now?"

'Yes," Gina said. "But you know what? Maybe not good idea from here with outdoor noises. It has to be quiet house atmosphere. Let's go back to hotel and we can use the empty chambermaid dressing room in back of hotel. Now no one is there."

"Perfect," I said. "You are some partner, Gina."

In that little room, with a table, a little sofa, and two chairs, we sat down and began our play.

As she began dialing, I said, "Let's hope she answers."

Then Gina stopped. She lowered the phone. My heart, it went in many directions, mostly down. She's chickened out at the last, the very last—there can't be any more last than this—minute.

I knew it. I knew it was too good to be true. Meeting an Italian girl who spoke English and was willing to be my unwitting co-conspirator. Of course, I didn't tell Gina that what she's doing is not only for Sofia but also for me. Actually, mostly for me. Now it's out the window. Gone was my deus ex machina. I saw Gina putting her phone down. I could swear that that warm little flame shaped like a marble that maybe did not exist, I could swear Sofia's warm gift was now marble cold.

"What's up?" I said, fearful. Didn't say: changed your mind?

"I had idea."

My vocal cords, where were they? But I raised my chin as if to say, Let's hear it.

"If I block the call, I don't have to make all the comments like I am talking from a borrowed phone and I don't have to say, Don't call me."

"You can block a call here? I thought that you can do that only in America."

"Every place is America. When you have a cell phone it's like America."

"Nicely said, Gina."

"So? Shall I? Or is it: should I?"

"Should, shall, makes no difference. Main thing is...sure. Go ahead. Let's hope she answers."

"She will. Here in Italy we love to talk on phone. We always answer the phone. Especially the women. We are very curious about who is calling. So I'll do it, okay?"

"Yes. Okay. Do it."

Gina dialed again. Once more my heart went—can't help saying it, I know it's not a writerly expression, but I'm being true to nature, describing precisely what happened, exactly how I felt, the worry, the anxiety, the fear, that's where my heart went—straight to my mouth.

I put my ear so close to Gina's cell phone I smelled her hair, a combination of musk and roses.

Heard ringing.

One.

Two.

Three.

Oh, no, Sofia is not picking up. How stupid of me. We didn't even discuss what to do if she didn't pick up. No, we won't leave a message. Can't. Impossible.

Four.

Now down, further down, my heart. Somewhere near my knees. Did you ever feel a heartbeat in your kneecaps?

I mouthed to Gina: "If no answer," and then made a shutting motion with both hands.

Gina nodded.

Five.

In mid-ring Sofia picked up.

An English translation of the conversation follows.

"Pronto." (By now everyone knows it means "hello.")

"Hello, is this Sofia?"

"Yes. Who is speaking?"

I gave a thumbs-up sign, and blew Gina a kiss.

"You don't know me by name. You just know me as Sandro's wife."

Silence. A silence so deep the air in that windowless little room seemed to move. Then it hung there. Heavy. Lugubrious. So thick it was palpable. A silence that needs no translation. A silence rendered in a universal tongue.

Then, finally, after a long while that seemed forever but probably lasted only five or six seconds, finally Sofia said:

"Yes...what is it you want to say, Signora Martinelli."

For a moment I imagined the surprise running through Sandro's wife's head as she hears Sofia call her Signora Martinelli, and then I remember it's Gina to whom Sofia is speaking. And then, back to reality, I imagine the shock, the trepidation, the absolute newness of events now going through Sofia's innards, her fears, her dreams, her dream fears being played out this very moment, and what she will feel like a couple of breaths from now when Gina says what the script tells her to say. And Sofia doesn't ask Signora Martinelli's name.

"I don't know how to begin, Sofia, if I may use your first name. You obviously know why I am calling. I...am...furious." Now Gina's voice became higher, sharper, and here a chill ran through me as I absorbed the drama of her tone, the pathos of her words. "And putting all this together, I conclude this has been going on behind my back for years. I'll say it again. I don't know how to begin. I just discovered this disgusting affair between the two of you. It's not important how I found out.

"That I don't have to tell you. Lovers are always careless. And then I understood his absences for which he always had some kind of explanation...So I just want to tell you, if this goes on one more day, ONE MORE DAY, and yes I am shouting, for I am shaken to my core, just one more day, I am taking the twins and running away and he'll never see the twins again. Maybe he doesn't care if he doesn't see me. But those twins he loves more than himself. Our lovely twins. More than life itself. In fact, I was thinking of killing myself and..."

"Please don't hurt yourself," Sofia interjected, her voice quavering. "Please. Please don't even think of that. I'm sorry."

"...and then he can raise the twins alone. That will keep him busy and maybe stop him from running from one woman to another. How can you do such a thing to me, to him, to you, to your husband?"

"I apologize, Signora Martinelli. You're right. In fact, I myself was thinking, no more. Of stopping. Of breaking off."

Round and round through my head went those last words like a happy, music-laden carousel.

"And this affair of my husband with you," Gina continued, "combined with the other disgusting matter, where he fools both of us, you and me. Two is too much. I don't know what I'm going to do with myself. I can't take it."

"Don't hurt yourself. I beg you... But wait. I hear you say *two*. Two? What's this about two? What do you mean two?"

"And I learn about these things, it's all compressed, like God's will, in one painful, anguished minute."

And then Sandro's wife...what am I talking about, Sandro's wife? Again Gina got me so into it I thought she was Sandro's wife. Gina began crying. She stopped speaking. She just cried into the phone. Now she looked at her little guide sheet. For the first time.

Sofia keeps saying, "I'm sorry, I'm sorry." Like an automaton she repeats those two words. "I'm sorry. I'm sorry. It will soon be better for you. I promise."

Through her tears, Gina says, "All this has to happen to me at once. Knocked on the head with a hammer. It fell out of his pocket. A piece of paper with the name of one of the secretaries from the insurance office here in Tabiano. With her private phone number decorated with those foul little hearts dancing all around the numbers and a little note to himself when he is going to see her. And your phone number too, And you say better. How better?"

"Oh my God," Sofia said.

"Everyone is deceiving everyone else," Gina said. "So no more, do you hear me? Answer me! Do you hear me?"

"I hear you. I'm sorry. I'm sorry. No more. No more."

Click. Gina hung up.

Her performance was so real, so convincing, I felt it was Sandro's wife berating Sofia, pouring her anger out on her.

"Wow," I said. "Bravo. Thank you, Gina. You were so convincing, I actually thought it was Sandro's wife talking to Sofia. Thank you so much." I was so moved by what Gina had done I couldn't resist hugging her, drawing her close, couldn't help kissing her hair. "What a performance. How did you think of the crying?"

"I felt Sandro's wife's pain."

"You did better even than in the rehearsal. How you said, knocked on the head with a hammer... How you put in, 'God's will...' And above all, how you cried. And you added that suicide bit. Unbelievable...boy, you're like a stage actress. Improvising. You put those little hearts around Sandro's girlfriend's phone number on that piece of paper. You were terrific."

"I cried because while talking I actually thought of myself as Sandro's wife. And from those movies I brought in that line with killing herself."

"Did you ever study drama, acting?"

"Never."

"You're a natural. Quite remarkable," I said, and I handed her a big American banknote.

She put her hands behind her back. "No. I am not taking anything for this."

I hugged her again and said, "You can't even imagine what you've achieved during these six-seven minutes. I think you liberated Sofia from a bind, a dilemma, a problem she was not capable of getting out of by herself. You freed her from a life-oppressing situation. You heard her say, no more. You heard her apologize and say, I'm sorry."

Gina closed her eyes for a moment and whispered, "Yes, yes."

"Okay," I told her, "you don't want any reward, and I can't thank you enough for your brilliant imagination. I...I just don't have words to express my gratitude. What you've accomplished is, simply put, a good deed. An enormously good, yes, even a great deed. And it's so nice of you to do this and not want any compensation for your good work. But here's an idea. May I take this sum that I have offered you and spend it on a fine dinner to which I am inviting you this evening, if you are free and willing?"

Gina looked straight at me. Not up, down, or to the side. I liked that look. It had a knowing, eye-sparkling brightness. And, in any case, she had just shown me how keen, smart, wise, astute she was.

"You are a good man," she said. "Helping out this Sofia lady. You are a man with a large heart. To spend so much money on flight and coming from New York to Italy. It is you who did good deed. I am admiring you for your kindness."

"But are you saying yes or no, Gina? Will a 'but' follow all your praise?"

She laughed. "No but. And yes. To your kind invitation. Yes. Gladly. But that is so much, too much money to spend on a dinner."

"You are worth it."

"Still too much. One can eat well without spending so much."

"Okay, part of it. I don't want you to feel uncomfortable."

Then Gina said, "Shall we meet here or..."

"Or...or..." I seemed to be following her hint. "shall I pick you up where you live? That would be more, how shall I put it, romantic?"

"Okay. That is good. Romantic. That is such a nice American word." And on the same little pad Gina had written some notes about her role, she chose a clean page, wrote down her address, and gave me the paper.

"It's not too far from here, in an apartment building. Apartment 4-G."

Wow, I thought, when Gina left. Can't believe it. That scenario that Gina revised, improved, expanded, is like out of a storybook. The pact between Sofia and Sandro is now, seemingly, broken. What Sofia had just heard from Gina gives her an out. And Sofia was saying, "Sorry. No more." Apologizing. And she will surely keep her word.

Sofia will probably bawl the hell out of Sandro. He will of course deny it. But maybe she won't contact him. Maybe Gina's call is enough for Sofia to stop. Maybe Sofia won't even tell Sandro that his wife called, a call the wife would deny if Sandro confronted her. Now that I think of it, it's quite likely Sofia won't say a word but will use Gina's call as the final push to the decision she's been postponing for so long. Plus that side affair of Sandro's, which probably hurts the most. Assuming Sofia brought it up, Sandro would deny that absolutely. Now if things proceed as they should, like a row of dominoes falling, it seems to me the book is closed.

ENDING 1

WE SAID HELLO WITH a hug, Sofia and me. And what a long hug it was. Thought it would never end. I did not want to let her go. Sofia too hugged me tight, kept whispering, "Thank you for coming. Thank you for coming." But it had to end, that hug, for I wanted to look at her face. Meanwhile, all I saw was the hair at the back of her head. But you know what? I did not bend forward to kiss her hello as I had bent forward last June to kiss her goodbye, with a friendly kiss on the temple. I was waiting for her to share some news. Figured she wouldn't be able to resist talking. Yet Sofia was absolutely silent. This made me wonder. I knew of course what had happened. So did she. But she didn't know I was the puppeteer.

Now we stood facing each other. Very close. The embrace not undone.

To my astonishment, Sofia began with, "Remember when we met by the beach here in Parma. What curious incidence that both of us we stay at the arts villa right across the street."

"Yes."

"Lives, they are full of coincidence."

I laughed and said, "Is that the first thing you have to say to me after all these months?"

My remark must have hit her, for she avoided my eyes and all she could say was:

"Truth is, I'm all mixed up..." She looked at me with a soft smile. "Please forgive me. I am so glad to see you."

"Me too," I said. "I'm so happy to hear that, Sofia."

She parted her lips, about to...but did not speak. She took a deep breath, exhaled. It sounded like a sigh. Maybe she *is* all mixed up. Off balance. This meeting with me right after her very likely break-up is a new, even awkward, experience.

Seeing Sofia's face before me, I said: "Sometimes there are questions we want to ask but we hold off asking them." I paused for a moment. But for this one I couldn't wait any longer. I had to ask. If she didn't volunteer, I would initiate the question: "A question like: So how are things?"

I saw Sofia tighten her lips.

"All right," I said. "Tell me later."

"I want to say it to you again, Giorgio. Thank you for coming. So good you are here."

Close to her face now, I was like a movie camera. Yes, I was focusing on Sofia's face, filming her, she looking more than ever like Sophia with a "ph," with her full, kissable lips parted in a smile, the flaring nostrils, high cheekbones, and those heart-devastating, signature green sloe eyes, now a strange mélange between hazel and brown, were glowing warmly.

Sofia still did not let go of that initial hug. In fact, I felt her closer to me as she said:

"Grazie. Grazie. Grazie mille per la tua assistenza benefica."

Sofia was thanking me for all the kind help I had given her.

And I replied, "My pleasure," but she didn't realize the full import of my two words.

"And I thank *you*, cara Sofia mia, for every bacio and abbraccio."

Sofia smiled. There was a little flame to that smile, a flame that reminded me of Sofia's gift. A smile soft and sunny and inviting. Little untouchable magnets hovered in that smile, and the glow in her green eyes a whisper that said, "Come closer."

And I did.

I bent forward and kissed the side of her throat. I didn't look up. I stayed there for a moment, pressing my lips into the soft skin, wondering if she would protest in any way, by word or movement of her hand or head, for this was not a neutral, friendly, platonic kiss, like my departing kiss this past June, a light kiss on her temple.

To my relief all she said was, "But that's not my temple."

Said with a flirtatious smile and the words rendered like a little song.

"What a memory you have, Sofia with an "f.""

Saying this, I raised my head and looked at her. Her happy smile now danced in her eyes. That smile was like a three-part canon; first, the song in her eyes, then the one on her lips, and the third when she spoke—one beautiful set of notes chasing another, but none of the three wishing to be caught, and so her eyes, her lips, her voice kept sending one little song after another.

"I'll be the judge," I said, "of where the desired house of worship is located. But if you insist on a kiss on your house of worship, I shall do it at once."

And I kissed her temple.

Sofia gazed—I could see the focus in her lenses, maybe I even saw a tiny image of myself—right into my eyes and said with mock seriousness: "In other words, Amadeo, you are master geographer."

First time I heard her pronounce the new name she had given me in her emails.

"Yes, Sofia, you see, my religious compass tells me where the various temples are. And where the most welcoming places for prayer."

Or maybe it ended this way:

ENDING **A**

LIKE A MAGICIAN, I made a little abracadabra motion with my right hand, touched my heart and returned the warm, marble-size little flame that Sofia had given me in Parma, in June. I did it by placing my hand on her heart and putting that gift of hers back whence it came.

"I kept it warm and safe and now, mia cara Sofia, it's yours again."

In my dream state, I seemed to see two things at once. All wrapped in that silken shawl of hers that a breeze gave wings and a gull flew away with.

After the embrace I saw Sofia's hand going to my heart. She placed her palm flat on my chest, made a grasping motion, then brought her hand back to her heart.

"It was just on loan, that flame," she said, "until I saw you again."

"So it was real after all. It wasn't a dream."

Sofia shook her head. But I didn't know if her "no" referred to "it was real after all," meaning it wasn't real. It *was* a dream. Or if her no was saying, "right, it wasn't a dream," it was quite real. Her gesture could have referred to one or the other.

"But the best house of worship is right here," I said.

I looked at her. She did not speak. Didn't have to. Her skin, her hair, spoke words. Her breath too, slow and measured, nostrils flaring, a quick quiver that sent me back to June, to Parma beach. No sounds, but words dense the way Sofia looked at me. The letters of everything she'd written, said, moved on the tiny black silken mantle of her retina. Her green sloe eyes, her flecked hazel eyes danced a welcome. Again her nostrils flared. In the space between her open, full, I once called kissable lips, flashed the moist glint of her teeth. A chill breeze from green-leafed forests cooled and fueled my fervor. Even her earlobes engaged, flushed and roseate.

I wonder if my—I purposely use this fancy, old-fashioned word—countenance mirrored hers. Did she see on me what I saw on her?

The next step was easy. Between us hummed, between us hovered a bond, ancient as the sea, a bond that preceded our births, silent, potent, overwhelming.

Happiness plucked at me. In the linotype of my mind, I saw tiny letters that spelled thank you in a dozen tongues.

I moved forward. An astral force, beyond hers, beyond mine, scended. On their own, our lips met.

She closed her eyes. Pressed into me.

"You don't know how happy I am you came, my little *fiammetta*," Sofia said into my ear and, as she spoke, her lips moved on my auricle. I felt each syllable vibrating like little kisses. "And you have to tell me everything about yourself, Amadeo. Everything. Starting with A."

At which I kissed her again.

And as I kissed her, I felt, the return—clear and brief as a bolt of lightning—of that now moist and warm little heart she had given me and taken back, intoxicating our lips, a welcome guest in this long-awaited feast I had tasted aforetime on the milk screen of my dreams.

And, at once, unbidden, I, with hands tied behind my back, undid as I had undone in my imagination many times, and following my silent command, Sofia too, after a slight forward movement of her shoulders and an alluring smile, put her hands behind her back and undid the orange strap of her bikini, revealing her full gorgeous breasts, pale in comparison to the rest of her suntanned skin, her smooth cinnamon shoulders, arms and upper chest.

I felt a quiver in Sofia, a palpable ecstasy, as if she was sensing something new.

A scent wafted out of her, dense like soft leather, as titillating to the nose as the touch of fine suede to fingertips.

On those lovely, pouting, sensual lips, just like her mother's, those luscious, full, sultry, kissable lips of the woman who—and no wonder—looked like Sophia L.

ABOUT THE PRESS

DZANC BOOKS is an award-winning independent press and a 501(c)3 nonprofit organization, created to advance unique idiosyncratic writing, to champion writers who don't fit neatly into the marketing niches of for-profit presses, and to publish debut and established authors of literary merit. In an industry increasingly driven by profits and a narrow field of bestsellers, Dzanc strives to remain a bastion of deep-thinking, original work and community outreach through our Writer-in-Residence programs, low-cost mentorship programs, and our robust internship program.

Dzanc's publishing initiatives and community programs are made possible through the invaluable support of state and federal grants and donations from corporations, foundations, and our dedicated community of readers and supporters who believe in the transformative power of the written word. Dzanc receives operational support from the national Endowment for the Arts (NEA), the Michigan Arts & Culture Council (MACC), ArtWorks.gov, and other benefactors.

Printed in the USA
CPSIA information can be obtained
at www.ICGtesting.com
JSHW020935130124
55333JS00007B/6